THE
THIRD DAY

*To Peter,
with my best wishes!*

[signature]

THE THIRD DAY

MARK B. RODDY

TATE PUBLISHING
AND ENTERPRISES, LLC

The Third Day
Copyright © 2014 by Mark B. Roddy. All rights reserved.

No part of this publication may be reproduced, stored in a retrieval system or transmitted in any way by any means, electronic, mechanical, photocopy, recording or otherwise without the prior permission of the author except as provided by USA copyright law.

This novel is a work of fiction. Names, descriptions, entities, and incidents included in the story are products of the author's imagination. Any resemblance to actual persons, events, and entities is entirely coincidental.

The opinions expressed by the author are not necessarily those of Tate Publishing, LLC.

Published by Tate Publishing & Enterprises, LLC
127 E. Trade Center Terrace | Mustang, Oklahoma 73064 USA
1.888.361.9473 | www.tatepublishing.com

Tate Publishing is committed to excellence in the publishing industry. The company reflects the philosophy established by the founders, based on Psalm 68:11,
"The Lord gave the word and great was the company of those who published it."

Book design copyright © 2014 by Tate Publishing, LLC. All rights reserved.
Cover design by Gian Philipp Rufin
Interior design by Jake Muelle

Published in the United States of America

ISBN: 978-1-63306-636-6
1. Fiction / Christian / Historical
2. Fiction / Religious
14.09.02

FOREWORD

The New Testament portion of the Bible contains a significant amount of information about Jesus Christ's passion, crucifixion, and resurrection. But it contains very little, if any information, as to the impact of these events on his family and his closest followers as well as the authority figures of the time.

I have sometimes wondered how Jesus's family and followers—these common yet extraordinary human beings—reacted to their entire world and beliefs being turned upside down as their charismatic and caring leader is suddenly arrested and executed like a common criminal. How did they then react when this same leader suddenly reappeared to them, raised from the dead?

My curiosity about their actions and reactions is the genesis for *The Third Day*. This is a fictionalized account of key figures involved in the crucifixion and resurrection storyline, of their thoughts and actions from the time of Jesus's crucifixion to the end of the day of his resurrection.

I have used the New Testament Gospel accounts of Matthew, Mark, Luke, and John as source material and have taken some "literary license" with the dialogue and compressed the timelines contained in their gospels. However, be assured that any changes I have made were done for the purposes of the storyline, not to alter or "rewrite" sacred scripture.

I would, therefore, hope any reader will see this book for that which it purports to be—one man's imagined perspective of the impact of these events on the lives of those who were close to, or came in contact with, Jesus as a result of his crucifixion, death, and resurrection.

—Mark B. Roddy

ONE

THE FIRST DAY

The two men pressed their backs as hard against the wall as they could, praying that they would blend in with the stones but hoping more realistically that the shadows were deep enough to hide them from the eyes of the six Roman soldiers who were marching by. Unbeknownst to the two men, however, the soldiers had their eyes and minds on something more important—their barracks and a delayed dinner. They were not in any mood to be further delayed in getting back to their quarters and washing away the blood and filth that inevitably was the souvenir from a crucifixion.

The three men whom the soldiers had crucified earlier that day had all been criminals according to Pilate, the procurator of Judea, and that was all they needed to know to carry out their orders. Unfortunately for the soldiers, all three had evidently been either inept or poor criminals as there was little in terms of possessions among the three for which the soldiers could cast lots. The biggest "prize" had been a homespun cloak worn by the one they had called Jesus, "the King of the Judeans." It was hardly a nobleman's robe, but it had

7

been won by the second-ranking member of the squad, Decanus Marcellus Centilla—his first crucifixion and his first prize. Now all they had on their minds was getting back to the barracks and cleaning up.

"Well, what do you think of your first crucifixion, Marcellus?" the centurion of the squad, Publius Gaius, said to his lucky subordinate.

"Not as bad as I'd imagined, Centurion Gaius." Marcellus looked down and held up the cloak he had won. "This isn't a bad souvenir either—the robe of a foreign king. Quite a prize for my first 'action,' wouldn't you say?" And all of them laughed.

"Yes, this one wasn't too bad. Sometimes the crowds get carried away, or the family tries to drag the criminals down from the cross. That can get messy. No, this one was kind of quiet, up until that storm later in the afternoon. If that Jesus fellow was the king of the Judeans, he must have been a pretty unpopular king. I've seldom seen as few people standing by a cross as this one." Gaius shook his head. "But that storm, by the gods, it sure made a mess of things—the mud and all. At least it washed the bodies down for us, so they were little less messy than usual."

Gaius was a hardened combat veteran. He had worked his way through the enlisted ranks, achieving the title and prestige of *centurion* based on a combat record which was second-to-none. His face had the consistency and texture of well-worn leather, owing to his many years in the field, and the many scars he bore and the slight limp with which he walked were testaments to his courage and fierceness. But his eyes, fierce as they initially seemed, also reflected an intelligent, thoughtful mind, one that followed orders without question but also frequently mulled over those orders and their consequences.

As Gaius continued to march his force toward the praetorium, his thoughts kept turning back to what he had just supervised. Two images kept coming back to him. The first was a composite image of the man called Jesus, who had been one of the three men his squad had executed. Though he loathed and despised anyone who wasn't a Roman, he had watched this man through his whole ordeal with what might be called a grudging respect. The man had remained calm and reserved throughout the day. Oh, he had groaned when he had fallen a couple of times enroute to the place of execution—a hill called Golgotha by the locals—and as they drove the nails into his body. But overall, Gaius had to admit that this man's demeanor was… He searched for a word that would sum up his perception. The only one which came to mind was "regal." He recalled in particular one of the man's comments. He closed his eyes briefly as he tried to remember what the man had said. "Yes, that's it. Something like 'Father, forgive them for they know not what they do.'"[1] Gaius remembered how he had looked around for someone who might be the man's father, but no such men were near the cross.

Then there was the woman who had stood at the foot of the cross and who had received the body of Jesus; he was struck by the way she too had acted throughout the crucifixion. She had cried when the body of the man whom Gaius assumed was a relative of hers—possibly her son—was placed in her lap. But he recalled there had been none of the loud weeping and wailing which so often accompanied the deaths of the condemned at crucifixions in this part of the world. No, she had remained quiet, obviously shaken and upset by the events, but she had remained in control of herself.

In fact, he was most bothered by the look she had given him as the body was placed in her lap. Not a look of hatred or condemnation but rather one which seemed to mirror the dead man's comments about his father forgiving them. When his soldiers placed the body in this woman's arms, he recalled the look she gave him seemed to say the same thing: "Do you know what you have just done?"

He shook his head to try and dispel the memory as he looked up at the now-clear sky, one that was darkening rapidly as evening fell on the land. "Well, at least it's clearing up now so tonight we won't have to deal with the infernal dampness that plagues this place." He looked at Marcellus again. "I tell you, Marcellus, before I got here, I always thought desert regions were dry. But this place, it gets so damp at times it will just wring the strength out of you. That's why that rain was so refreshing this afternoon, really cooled things down."

The men found themselves at the gates of the praetorium. While it was the residence and formal offices of Pilate, their quarters were attached to one of the large courtyards that also served as their training grounds and assembly area. Gaius nodded toward Pilate's chambers. "You men go and clean up. I need to report to Pilate. Remember this, Marcellus. Don't ever bother cleaning up before you go see Pilate after any task he gives you. He's always suspicious of clean soldiers."

The five men saluted their leader and turned left toward their quarters as Gaius turned right and headed toward Pilate's formal chamber. He nodded and bowed slightly in deference to Antonius Septimus, Pilate's chief scribe and confidante. He was known unofficially by the cohort of soldiers as the gatekeeper as you didn't get in to see Pilate unless you reported to Septimus first. It was he who decided who and what was brought to the procurator's attention. Septimus was also known as "spiritus turbulentus: the fussy ghost" among the soldiers, owing to his dislike of anything related to dirt and muck, and his extremely pale complexion. They would joke behind his back that when Septimus was wearing a white tunic it was hard to tell where the tunic began and his skin stopped.

Unlike his superior, Septimus would have much preferred the soldiers clean up before presenting themselves to Pilate. He was often nauseated by the blood on the men's uniforms and the smell that went with the blood and whatever else had stained the man's cloak and armor. But Pilate, a man with no real military experience, reveled in the muck. It made him feel closer to the action as if he too had taken place in the conflict, even if the "battle" pitted six men armed with swords, lances, nails, hammers, and a cross against an unarmed naked man.

"Hail, Septimus."

"Hail, Centurion." Septimus never bothered to learn the names of the soldiers; he could just barely

11

distinguish their ranks. "What business have you here this evening?"

"I am here to report to Pilate on the completion of the execution of the criminals, which included the insurrectionist Jesus."

"Oh, yes, him, the so-called king of the Judeans. Wait here, please. I do know Pilate wanted to hear about this." Septimus turned and started to walk into Pilate's formal chamber but then stopped and turned to face the soldier. "Centurion, when you report, please be brief. Our lord Pilate has an engagement this evening, and he does not have a lot of time to spare."

"As you command, sir," Gaius responded. Septimus cast him a cold stare. He sensed a tone of condescension and insubordination in the other man's tone of voice. However, he was not that good a reader of people to be sure, so he just gave the centurion his most withering glance, sniffed, and turned his back on the other man, walking through the curtains into Pilate's office. That left Gaius with a wry smile on his face and a slight shake of his head as he considered the arrogance and ignorance of the scribe. *I wonder if he plays dice. He's so stupid and easy to read I could make a fortune off of him.*

As he waited, his mind started to drift back again to the face of the woman at the foot of the cross. Try as he might, he could not forget the look she had given him. It was haunting; not in a scary way, but in a way which now seemed seared in his mind. His thoughts were broken by Septimus parting the curtains in as dramatic a fashion as he could muster and sweeping his arm from Gaius toward the opening, indicating it was time for his audience with Pilate.

Gaius straightened his posture, tugged at the lower edge of his lorica segmentata armor, and walked past Septimus, nodding slightly as he did so. Again, Septimus could not read the gesture as being one of respect or contempt. Pilate was standing behind a table, looking at one of several scrolls spread out on it. Gaius stood at attention before the desk and placed his right arm and fist across his chest as he saluted the representative of the divine emperor in Judea, Pontius Pilate. "Hail Pilate, procurator of Judea."

Pilate looked up from his scrolls and nodded at the centurion's salute. "Report, Centurion," was all he said as he looked away toward Septimus, who was standing several feet behind and to one side of Gaius, ready to take in all the centurion had to report. This was standard procedure for Pilate, and Gaius had been through this routine several times before. Nevertheless, as a soldier, it made him nervous to have another man whom he could not fully see but who he knew was relatively close to him, standing behind him.

"Sir, as I am sure you already know, the three criminals have been executed, and their bodies taken down from the crosses. There was no trouble. We turned two of the bodies over to the citizens who run the pauper's cemetery. The other one, the body of the 'king of the Judeans,' was turned over to a man, Joseph by name, who presented us with a warrant from your office for the body." A chill went up Gaius' spine. He suddenly realized he had not considered the possibility

Pilate may have not authorized this act and that he'd given the body to someone without official permission. Pilate's comment took care of his fear.

"Yes, Joseph of...of..." Pilate looked at Septimus. "Where was this Joseph from again?"

"Arimithea, my lord. Joseph of Arimithea."

"Yes, that's it. Arimithea." Pilate looked back at the centurion. "Anything else to report?" Gaius shifted slightly on his feet.

"If I may make a suggestion related to security, sir." Pilate looked at Gaius. He didn't really know too many of his soldiers, at least not as well as he thought he should. But he'd heard enough about Gaius to know he was a loyal soldier and a true Roman, someone who, more or less, could be trusted to have the interests of Rome ahead of his own.

"Go ahead, Centurion."

"Well, sir, we know this man Jesus had some devoted followers. I don't know too much about them, but I was wondering if we should go out and arrest them as well, just to ensure they don't cause you or the empire any more trouble." Pilate who had had his back to the Centurion turned to look at him and smiled. He took a few steps toward Gaius then stopped far enough away to be just out of range of any stench and filth on the other man.

"How many of his followers were at the crucifixion today, Centurion?" Gaius thought for a minute or so, trying to recall those people who had obviously been at the site because of some sort of a relationship to Jesus.

"Well, sir, there were several women there. But now as I recall, there was only one, maybe two men, there. They seemed to be focused on taking care of the women, particularly the one who I think was one of the criminals' mother." Her look flashed through his mind again.

Pilate smiled again. "Exactly, Centurion, one or two out of a band of how many? Ten to twenty? Cut off the head of the snake, and the rest of the snake dies and is of no further threat to you. As far as we know, the others have scattered to the four winds. They abandoned their leader, so I doubt we have anything much to fear from them.

"No, your men have had enough action for today. I think we will see little, if anything, from these followers of this dead Jesus. He is gone. They are too. Now bathe, rest, and eat, Centurion, with my thanks for a job well done."

"Thank you, my lord Pilate. By your leave," he said as he saluted. Again, Pilate nodded in response.

"You have our leave to go, Centurion." Gaius turned around smartly and went through the opening provided once more by Septimus's arm. He nodded again at Septimus, who nodded back, acknowledging the compliment which had been paid to him by Pilate. Septimus then walked closer to Pilate, awaiting further instructions.

"Septimus"—Pilate nodded towards the door— "this centurion is a good man, a good Roman. But I sense some, some, well, I am not sure what to call it; some slight concern on his part over this whole matter."

"I didn't notice anything, my lord Pilate," Septimus responded. Pilate smiled.

That's why you're a scribe and I am the Procurator, Septimus, he thought. Pilate frowned slightly and then rubbed his face. "It was very subtle, Septimus, probably nothing at all. This 'Jesus affair' has worn me out. Perhaps I am sensing things that are not there." Pilate looked up at the other man, expressionless, which made Septimus a little uncomfortable. "At any rate, make sure *his* report matches our report on this incident. It was our forces who uncovered this traitor and rebel, Jesus. That we captured him and swiftly administered Roman justice to stamp out any threat to Roman authority in Judea. Rome need not know this Jesus was actually brought to us by a bunch of the local religious leaders who appeared to be more jealous of him than anything."

"I will, my lord. Anything else?"

"Yes, what of that criminal whom I released today instead of this Jesus? What was his name?"

"Barabbas, sir. He's been a troublemaker for some time."

"Well, see to it he troubles us no longer after tomorrow, Septimus. The 'victors' get to write the history, and I want us to be the author of today's events, not some criminal who was released for what I consider to be the wrong reasons."

"I will see that it is taken care of, my lord Pilate. Anything else, sir?"

"Yes, are my clothes and escort ready for my dinner with Herod?"

"They are, my Lord. He is expecting you within the hour."

Pilate smiled. "Then I have two hours in which to get ready. Please have some wine brought in. We will celebrate the end of another traitor to Rome."

TWO

The two men in the shadows, Philip and James, breathed a sigh of relief after the soldiers passed. They looked at each other, nodded, and then carefully made their way down several side streets in Jerusalem, heading for the inn and the room where they had dined the night before. As it was the eve of the Sabbath, and a Passover Sabbath at that, the streets were quite empty. Even as the two tried to appear as nonchalant as they could, every glance their way by anyone raised their anxiety. Right now, to them everyone was a threat. After several more of what they considered to be close calls with other Roman patrols and one almost encounter with some temple guards, they found themselves knocking on the door of the upper room where they had last been altogether with the friend and leader, Jesus.

"Yes?" was the reply to their knocking.

Without raising his voice, James answered, "Philip and James." The door was unlocked and opened just far enough to let the two men in then swiftly closed behind them. Their friend, Thomas, was the one handling the door.

"Did anyone see you come here?" Thomas asked a little too sharply as far as James was concerned. But then he realized they were all on edge.

"No, not as far as I can tell, Thomas." Philip nodded his head in agreement with James's statement. James looked around at the darkening room; only a few lights were on. It was nowhere near as bright or as festive as it had been early the night before when the twelve sat with their friend and leader, Jesus, for the Passover seder. Only a few lamps were burning, probably no more than a third of the ones in the room. The room looked much as it had when they had arrived for the seder the night before. The only thing that seemed to be missing was one of the cups from the center of the table. Despite the lack of light, James was able to count nine figures, including himself, all male. He particularly noted Peter, who was sitting by himself in a corner of the room. He was leaning heavily on a table, his back partially turned to the rest of the men.

James started an inventory of who was there and who was missing. He soon determined that his brother John, Judas, and Simon were not there. He looked around as the other disciples of Jesus sat looking at each other. He could only think that what he saw was a combination of fear and confusion as all of them tried to make sense of what had occurred over the last twelve hours or so. "Has anyone seen John? Or Judas, or Simon?" he asked of no one in particular. That caused most of the others, but not Peter, to look around; some of them realizing for the first time that not all twelve of them were back in the room. Matthew was the first to speak up.

"Um, I think that John has gone to the home of Joseph of Arimithea. I was at the, ah, the crucifixion, and I heard Jesus say something to John and Mary. And after that, John put his arm around Mary and started to shelter her somewhat from the sight of...of Jesus hanging there." He shook his head and continued, "But she would have nothing of it. She just stood there, looking at her son dying, and not making a sound." He shook his head again. "I just don't understand. What has happened?" Matthew looked around as if one of his colleagues might have the answer, but they were all just as dumbfounded as was he.

James spoke again, "What about Judas or Simon? Does anyone know what happened to either of them? If they get caught, they might lead the Romans here to us."

This time, it was Andrew, Peter's brother, who spoke. "I think Simon has gone to the house of his cousin who lives on the edge of the city. It's an out-of-the-way place. He should be safe there. As for Judas, I have no idea. The last time I saw him was in the garden when he went up to Jesus and kissed him." As Matthew had done before, Andrew looked around at the others. "Do any of you know what that was all about anyway? Why Judas kissed Jesus?"

Now it was Nathaniel's turn to speak. "It was a kiss of betrayal. That's what it was!" He noticed the others look up as he spoke these words. "Don't you remember? It was right after that the guards ran up and seized Jesus. Then Peter tried to save him and cut one of the men who was standing by Jesus, didn't you,

Peter?" Peter sat still, not moving, not saying anything. The only way anyone would have been able to tell Peter was alive was by noticing the way he slowly turned the cup he held in his large, gnarled hands, the hands of a working fisherman. James recognized it as the cup which had been at the center of the table—at the place where Jesus sat.

Philip spoke up. "Just before I met up with James on our way here, I passed by a couple of the temple guards. They were talking about someone who had just hanged himself, and I heard them mention Judas's name."

"No!" Nathaniel exclaimed. "Is that possible? Is it possible that the betrayer of Jesus has killed himself?" That started some level of excited conversation among them all. The chatter came to an end when Peter finally broke his silence.

"Judas wasn't the only one who betrayed Jesus," he said as he continued to turn and stare at the cup in his hands. "We all betrayed him." The silence following Peter's comment was palpable as the truth of what he said sank in. The others knew the only ones who had stayed with Jesus as he was led away were Peter and John. The rest of them had scattered just like the sheep Jesus had been so fond of using in his parables.

None of the other nine knew what had happened at the courtyard of the high priest, how John had been able to get in to the inner courtyard and watch the interrogation of Jesus from a distance, just out of hearing range. Peter had stayed in the outer courtyard and eventually left the facility in fear of his life after vehemently denying that he knew Jesus. It was only after he heard the cock crow did he realize what he had done, and the gravity and shame of his denials now weighed on him as surely as if a huge rock had been placed on his shoulders.

"Well," Nathaniel said, breaking the silence. "I still say that whatever any of us did or think we did, Judas was a traitor. After all the Master had done for us, done for him, to turn him over to those who eventually gave him to the Romans to kill. If Judas is dead, then I say it is God's will, and blessed be God for this." While the others might have been thinking similarly strong thoughts about Judas, they were all still somewhat surprised anyone had the nerve to speak out and say what each of them was thinking. An awkward silence once again fell on the room. And again, it was Peter who broke the silence.

"It is not for us to judge anyone, Nathaniel. Remember what the Master said when the crowd wanted to stone Mary Magdalene not so long ago. 'He that is without sin among you, let him first cast a stone at her.'[2] Right now, I don't think any of us could be judged to be without sin."

"Even you, Peter, who followed the Master to the court of the high priest?"

Peter never took his eyes off the cup. "Yes, Nathaniel, most especially me." Nathaniel made a motion to ask Peter what he meant, but by Peter's body language, nothing more was going to be forthcoming from him on this topic. So Nathaniel just looked around, shook his head, and lapsed into the same silence that enveloped all of his companions.

22

Thomas had not left his post at the door. Thomas was a big man, almost as big as Peter, and he had taken it upon himself to act as the guardian of the door. If the Romans wanted them, they would have to get by him, first, he had thought to himself as he leaned against. the door. Despite his seeming bravery, however, he too was overcome with doubts and questions about the activities of the last half day.

There was a prolonged silence after Peter's reply to Nathaniel, each man lost in his own thoughts and fears. As Thomas looked over the nine men, he once again asked aloud the question all of them were thinking. "What has happened? Why did they kill Jesus? After all the good he'd done, why? It just does not make any sense. He was no threat to anyone, certainly not to the Romans. I mean look at us. Could we ever be considered to be a band of dangerous renegades or revolutionaries? Half of us do not carry any kind of sword, and those that do, I suspect, would not last very long against real soldiers.

"Jesus was always talking of peace and how we must love our neighbors. He cured sick people. I never heard him speak ill of anyone. So why was he killed? What did he do to deserve such a death?"

Peter looked up from his studying of the cup. Although he was in a state of deep self-pity and shame, his natural leadership abilities, or what some might call his impetuousness, led him to realize his companions were searching for answers that none of them could provide. Yet, it did none of them any good to wallow in confusion as well as, in his case, self-pity.

He carefully placed the cup on the small side table next to where he had been seated, stood up, and turned to face the others. Immediately, all eyes were upon him, waiting for him to explain what they had witnessed, to make sense of it all. He looked down at his hands and then once again at the eight faces fastened on him. Despite the relatively low light in the room, he could make out each man's face, having spent so much time with them in all kinds of places and events over the last three years. His recollections of those times initially lightened his mood, but then he started thinking about all Jesus had done for them and others, and most especially how he had called out Peter to be their leader, and the thought just deepened his gloom and guilt.

Nevertheless, the others were looking for answers, and even if he had no real answers to provide, Peter felt he had to say something. "My friends, my, my brothers, I can't answer the why of what we've gone through—of all that Jesus went through today. I have no special vision or words which Jesus told me, which I can share with you to help ease your pain and doubts. I heard and have tried to grasp the same messages he shared with all of you. Tried to see if I can draw any meaning from what he told us and how that might relate to what we have all witnessed today." He looked around the room again then at his hands. "I keep thinking about what he said, particularly this last week or so. I keep trying to see if there was something there we missed, where we could have taken some action to prevent this.

"Yet I also recall when he mentioned his death once and I stated he should be spared such a fate, he gave me a verbal lashing that still stings when I think about it." Peter silently recalled that conversation with Jesus. He suddenly realized Jesus was not angry with him as much as he was disappointed with the comment Peter had made. Disappointment then, and now he knew he had disappointed Jesus again. He shook his head and fought back the tears. The others just assumed he too was overcome with grief at the loss of their Master. That was part of it, but other emotions were raging within Peter as well. He fought to control his thoughts and looked up at the group again.

"I don't know. It's almost like he, like he felt he had to die. To…to achieve some greater purpose. I also suspect whatever that purpose is, or was, he told us about it in one of his talks with us." He stopped and shook his head. "Whatever he might have told us though, right now I just cannot tie it to what we all witnessed, what he went through today. I sense the answer is there somewhere. But my friends, my brothers, I cannot, at least now, figure out what the message or purpose is or was. I'm sorry." He sat down wearily, once again focusing on his hands as if somehow they might divine an answer for him.

Thomas broke the silence. "Well, if we can't figure that out, we need to figure out what we do to stay alive. We cannot stay in this room forever. Sooner or later, someone is going to remember they saw us here in the last couple of days and come looking for us.

"Should we stay here, just waiting? Should we scatter and return to our own villages? What? What should we do? What do you all think we should do?"

Peter looked up. Now he sensed fear was replacing doubt, and he knew from his own life experiences scared men could do stupid things. "I think for tonight we should stay here," he said. The others looked at each other, trying to sense any affirmation of Peter's plan. "Think about it. The Romans have had plenty of chances to arrest us if they wanted to. They could have grabbed all of us in Gethsemane. They could have picked up John and me at the courtyard of the high priest." He cast his eyes down as he again recalled his denial of Jesus and how he then ran away from that place. But he continued. "Apparently, they did not bother with John or Matthew when they were crucifying Jesus."

He shook his head as he walked slowly among his companions. "No, I think it is best if we stay together." He pointed at the floor. "Stay together here, at least for tonight. Then one of us can go out tomorrow and try and figure out if we are wanted men or not." The others nodded in agreement. It was not much of a plan, but it seemed to be the best one they could come up with for now. "It has been a long day for all of us. I don't know what tomorrow will bring, but for now, I would suggest you all try and rest."

"And pray," added Thaddeus, who, up until now, had been silent. Peter turned to look at his friend.

"Yes, you are right, Thaddeus. We should pray. We failed at that in the garden last night, perhaps we can do better tonight." As all shook their heads in agreement, each man moved apart to have some modicum of privacy, pulled his prayer shawl over his head, and started— silently for most, as a whisper for some—to pray.

THREE

"How is she, John?" Joseph of Arimithea was speaking to one of his guests—John, who had accompanied Jesus's mother, Mary, after Joseph had arranged the burial of Jesus in a tomb not far from where he had died.

"She is resting, Joseph. Her strength of character is amazing. What she saw today, all she has gone through…" John shook his head. "Despite all that, she seems to have this…this…I don't know what to call it, Joseph. It's like an inner peace. It's as if she sees a greater purpose in Jesus's death." John looked down at the floor and then back at his host. "I would very much like to have that same hope in my heart. I've tried to recall all the things our Master said, trying to see if I can find that seed of hope Mary seems to have found. Right now, though, I am having trouble finding it."

Joseph put his hand on the other man's shoulder. "It has been a long and trying day, John, for all of us. I too see her strength, and I too yearn for some meaning in all of this." He sighed. "But to be honest, I am too tired and filled with grief to think clearly right now. Perhaps the morning will bring some clarity to our thoughts." He looked around his house and then back at John.

"You and Mary are safe here. No one will bother you tonight. Rest and let us see what tomorrow brings."

John nodded wearily. "That is sound advice, Joseph. Thank you for that and for your hospitality. It means much to me, and I'm sure it does to Mary as well," he said as he nodded in the direction of the room where he had left Mary. "The Master once said, 'Take therefore no thought for the morrow: for the morrow shall take thought for the things of itself. Sufficient unto the day is the evil thereof.'[3] Never were truer words spoken." John bowed slightly toward his guest, looked once more in the direction of Mary's room, and started off in the direction of the room to which one of Joseph's servants now led him.

For his part, Joseph sighed again and shook his head as he tried to make some sense of all that had occurred this day but, like so many others, was unable to do so. After a minute or two, he walked off toward his library. He ensured the door was closed after he entered it and walked toward the table where something lay wrapped in a white cloth, a cloth which also bore some wet spots as if it held something that had been washed but not dried.

Indeed, that was what it was—the crown of thorns which had been forced onto Jesus's head by the soldiers prior to his crucifixion. Joseph carefully unwrapped it and used the cloth to finish drying off the item he had hastily washed with some of the water brought in to the tomb to wash Jesus's body as part of its burial preparation. Joseph had overseen this action personally, ensuring Mary and John were not in the tomb during this somewhat-grisly task but were allowed in after the body had been fully but quickly prepared for burial. As he gently wiped off the last vestiges of water, he cried, thinking of his dead friend and of how his mother had cried as she seemingly bid a final farewell to her son.

And yet, like John, he had seen something in her eyes that seemed to say "all is not lost." He tried to hold on to that thought as he finished drying the woven headpiece, but exhaustion overtook his mind, and he had to struggle to rewrap it in a fresh cloth and place it high upon one of the shelves that held some of the many scrolls populating the room in which Joseph now stood. Finishing his task, he wearily sat down and almost immediately fell asleep.

Mary sat in the dark in her room. She too was going over all of the events of the last day as well as all of the events of her life with Jesus, starting with the visit by the angel when she was still a young single girl engaged to the carpenter Joseph. She had spent a lifetime pondering all the events related to her only child. That, combined with the time she and Jesus had spent alone talking as he grew up and whenever he visited her during his ministry as an adult, had given her much to think about.

She recalled the old man Simeon when she and Joseph had first presented her son in the temple. He had said Jesus was destined to be the rise and fall of many in Palestine. Now she tried but could not quite rationalize those comments with the events of the past twelve hours or so when she saw her son executed like a common criminal. Yet upon his cross was a sign declaring him the "king of the Judeans."

She also recalled how three strangers had visited her family when Jesus was still an infant. Why and how these three men of property and education had come seeking Jesus was something that still puzzled her. But she also remembered how soon after their visit, Joseph, Jesus, and she had to flee the country to save her son's life. *Why was he spared then, to die such a seemingly ignominious death today? After all the good he had done, starting with the wedding at Cana*, she thought to herself.

The wedding at Cana. She smiled as she recalled that singular event. How she had approached Jesus, feeling he could somehow solve the potentially embarrassing issue of the bride and groom not having enough wine for all their guests. Mary laughed softly and shook her head as she remembered her not asking Jesus for his help but how she just told him, "They have no wine,"[4] and his reply, "Woman, what have I to do with thee? mine hour is not yet come."[5]

Oh, yes, it has, son, she had thought to herself at the time as she had smiled at him, patted him lovingly on the cheek, and then turned and told the wedding stewards to do whatever he tells you. She smiled again as the image of Jesus standing there shrugging his shoulders as if to say "How can any son turn down his mother?" appeared sharp and clear in her memory.

Today, the roles had been reversed somewhat as Jesus had told her to take John as her new "son" and for John to take care of his mother. She closed her eyes to try and blot out that memory, but it was still too fresh and raw to be fully expunged. Her son was dead, killed in a most horrible manner.

However, despite her grief, she still felt somehow this was not the end so many others seemed to think it was. The more she pondered all the events of her own life and those of her son, the more she became convinced that, for reasons she could not fully form or express to herself, there was yet more. How that could be, she really could not fathom, particularly as fatigue had started to set in and dull her senses. Her mind became clouded as, despite her best efforts to stay awake and try and reason things out, her body just could not fight the sleep that cut off the thoughts and confusion. She fell asleep with her last conscious thought being that, despite how illogical it might seem, today really didn't represent the end of Jesus.

FOUR

Herod Antipas, the tetrarch of Galilee, was a vain and pompous man, very much enamored with the prerequisites of his office. He fancied himself as a real ruler even though all his limited authority emanated from Rome and was controlled, in particular, by Pontius Pilate. Herod had no use for Pilate as an individual but was smart enough to realize his own continued existence rested solely on the whims of the Roman procurator. Therefore, despite his own contempt for the man, Herod made sure to call on Pilate whenever he was in Jerusalem and to always hold a banquet in his honor during such visits.

Thus it was that Herod waited—impatiently—for his dinner guest to arrive. He liked to drink but refrained from doing so until Pilate, who was always late for these events, had arrived. It was bad form to greet the procurator in anything less than a fully sober state. After the anticipation and subsequent disappointment Herod had experienced when Pilate sent Jesus to Herod earlier in the day and Jesus's total silence during the "audience" with Herod, he was ready for wine, a lot of wine. But not until Pilate arrived.

At last, over an hour late, Pilate arrived begging Herod's forgiveness for being so tardy. Neither man was fluent in the other's native tongue, so most of their conversations took place through translators. That further slowed the entourage's movement toward the banquet hall, but eventually, the guest of honor and his host found themselves seated behind a large and magnificent display of food: fresh fruits and vegetables, cured meats and fish, and much wine. Both men toasted the health of the other, and all rose to toast the health of the divine emperor, Tiberius Caesar.

Herod was enjoying himself while, at the same time, noticing that the usually reticent Pilate was even less communicative than normal. This both worried and confused Herod, neither condition being aided by the copious amounts of wine he was now consuming. As the evening wore on, Herod decided the best course of action was to significantly reduce his intake of wine, at least until Pilate left, which, if the procurator followed his normal pattern, would occur in a very short period of time. The tetrarch sensed Pilate had something to discuss with Herod, aggrandizing in his own mind the value Pilate placed on the tetrarch's advice. In reality, most of their "discussions" were more like lectures, with Pilate doing the talking and Herod, the listening.

Tonight was no different. As he got up to leave, Pilate motioned to Herod he wanted to have a private conversation with him. That meant the four men—the two principals and each of their translators—would move to a side room away from the noise of the party and the prying ears of Herod's spies, which Pilate knew Herod had liberally sprinkled among the guests at the dinner. Once they were alone, Pilate motioned for Herod to sit next to him on one of the couches in the small side room. The translators stood behind their two charges, ready to convey the words, if not the meaning, of their respective masters' comments, with both of them knowing from previous experience Pilate's translator would be doing most of the talking.

"Herod, my friend, today we put to rest another potential rebellion when we crucified that Jesus, whom I branded as the 'king of the Judeans.' However, it disturbs me greatly he was brought before us not by your guards or your operatives but by the local religious leaders." Herod started to speak in protest, but Pilate's upturned hand stopped him before he could say a word.

"Now I really don't care why these religious leaders brought this man to me. My sense is he really wasn't a rebel or a traitor, but that is of no importance. He served a purpose for me. I was able to demonstrate the power of Rome and its willingness to crush any and all who might threaten it in any way." Pilate leaned forward, staring hard at Herod. "What does concern me, however, is that from what I have learned, this man was running around the countryside for some number of years, meeting with all kinds of people and could have just as easily been stirring up trouble. And as I said earlier, the first I learned of him is from some local religious leaders.

"Then when he was in the Praetorium, these same people tried to stir up the population in some sort of a riot. Fortunately, there were not many of their followers there, so my soldiers were able to easily keep the situation under control. But it could have turned ugly, Herod, and that would have displeased me. It would have displeased Rome.

"You 'rule,' Herod, by and with Rome's pleasure. That means you owe your allegiance and your life to us—to me, in fact, as Rome's duly appointed official in this province. I expect to learn of rebels and fanatics of any kind from you, not from the local citizenry. I do not want to be surprised by another 'Jesus' or any other like him being brought to my, and Rome's, attention by anyone other than you or one of your minions. Do I make myself clear?"

All Herod could do in response was feebly shake his head yes as he now regretted having drunk so much wine earlier. *What might I have missed in what he just said?* he wondered.

Pilate stood up. "Good, then we will have no more talk of this unpleasantness, and I look forward to no more surprises as much as I look forward to your next banquet when you return to Jerusalem for another visit. Until then, hail Caesar! Good night to you, Tetrarch Herod."

"Hail Caesar," was the other man's feeble reply as the gravity of what he had just been told—no, threatened with—sank in, as did the anger of being so humiliated in front of one of his subordinates, his translator. *I suspect, in ten minutes, this conversation will be all over the house*, he thought to himself as he gave the translator a withering look, hoping that might be enough to scare the man into silence. It would not.

FIVE

Mary Magdalene could not stop crying. Never had anyone treated her as kindly as had Jesus. Never had any man looked at her as he had—not as an object of desire or lust, but as a whole person. Someone with worth. Someone who was the equal of any other human being on the earth.

Not too long ago, Jesus had saved her from death by stoning, and he had set her feet on a path away from her life as a prostitute. She had subsequently witnessed many of his other acts of kindness particularly focused on the downtrodden and marginalized members of the Judean society. And now, for reasons she could not comprehend, he was dead—dead at the hands of the Romans for crimes. *Crimes? What crimes?* she asked herself. *For being kind to people like me? For taking care of those who were in need? Why? Why?*

But no answers were forthcoming, only the tears. Tears like the ones she had shed on his feet when, after she had been able to absorb the enormity of what Jesus had done in saving her from the mob that wished to kill her, she had washed his feet with her tears and dried them with her hair. What was it he had said that day not so long ago when one of his followers—she couldn't remember which one—had complained about her wasting the oil she'd used that afternoon in her act of what she could only call an adoration of Jesus. Yes, he'd said something about how she was anointing him in preparation for his death and burial.

She looked up in horror. Could she have somehow contributed to what had just occurred by doing something that had cursed Jesus or caused bad luck to fall upon him? That further deepened her grief until something deep inside her told her such thoughts were nonsense. Nevertheless, the thought she had nothing to do with his death brought little joy. Jesus was dead; his followers had scattered, and she had no idea where his mother was, although she had seen John leading Mary away from the tomb where the older rich man— what was his name? She could not recall it. But it was from where that older rich man had led the burial party, where they had buried Jesus in a cave-like tomb not too far from where he had died. She remembered now, as the large stone was rolled over the opening, John had taken Mary away, following the old man, and the others following them. All except Mary Magdalene. She had stayed at the grave until she saw the guards coming.

As she had hurried away, she had heard them laughing and complaining about having to guard a dead man to keep him from walking away. It was all too confusing for this woman who had singularly attractive looks and a personality willing to please people in any way in a vain hope of winning their friendship. As she thought back on her life, she now realized that while she had had many acquaintances, she did not have any real friends until she met Jesus. And this friendship had lasted but a few months. Despite its brevity, Mary Magdalene knew he had changed her perspective on life enough so that looking for "friendships" was not important to her anymore. She also now had little concern she would allow herself to go back to her old ways of "making friends."

No, she felt; despite her grief, there was something else in store for her. But she could not see the way at this moment because her guide and her friend, Jesus, was gone. As with so many others that day, she was left with confused and fractured thoughts of what had happened, what had gone wrong, and what was to going to happen now that Jesus was dead.

SIX

THE SECOND DAY

The nine men woke from a night of fitful sleep to knocking on the door of the room. Thomas shook the sleep from his body and bolted for the door, ready to take on whoever might be on the other side. He relaxed somewhat when he recognized the voice of the owner of the inn, Joseph of Arimithea. But he was also concerned as Joseph was a member of the Sanhedrin, the group which had turned Jesus over to Pilate. Perhaps this was a trick to get them to open the door so the temple guards could burst in and seize them all. Thus, despite the other man's pleadings, he resisted opening the door.

It was only when Peter walked over to the door that Thomas considered relenting. "It's Joseph. Joseph of Arimithea, Peter."

"You recognize his voice?"

"Yes, I do."

"Then let him in," Peter said as he raised his arm and pointed to the door.

"But, Peter," Thomas whispered, "he's one of them—the Sanhedrin! The ones who turned Jesus over to the

Romans! He might have temple guards with him. Come to arrest us."

Peter looked at Thomas and then turned to look at the other seven men, who were all now standing close by and exhibiting a combination of fear and resignation. He then turned to look at the door. "Joseph, this is Peter. Are you alone?"

"No, Peter," the voice from the other side replied. "I have two servants with me who have brought you food and drink and who need to clean up the room." Peter again pointed to the door.

"There, you see? He is not alone. Open the door, Thomas, and let the owner of this place in, and let peace come in with him."

Thomas hesitated for a minute, but the growing exasperation in Peter's face overtook his own concerns, and he unbarred the door, at the same time keeping his body against it as he opened it so he could hopefully close it again quickly if there were temple guards in the hallway. As soon as the door was opened enough to let one pass, Joseph entered the room, followed by his two servants. He looked to his right at Thomas, nodded slightly to him, and then looked for and found Peter. "Peace be to you and all in this room, my friends," Joseph said as he nodded at Peter and then looked at the other men.

"Peace to you, Joseph." Peter sheepishly looked around the room, which was definitely in need of a cleaning, and added, "And thank you for allowing us to stay here last night. We had nowhere else to go, and we, well, we were afraid to go out and back to...Well,

I don't know where we would have gone. We were afraid." Joseph smiled slightly and put his hand on the other man's shoulder, although it took some effort as Peter stood a good head taller than Joseph.

"I understand, Peter. I'm glad you all made it back here." He looked around and counted the nine. He knew that John was at his house, and he had already heard what had happened to Judas, although he wondered if the men in the room were aware of his death. "I only count nine, Peter. John is at my house with Mary." He looked down and then back at Peter. "Have you heard what happened to Judas?"

Peter nodded. "One of our number heard some temple guards talking last night as he was on his way here. Then it is true, Judas killed himself?"

"Yes, it is true, Peter. But that still leaves one of you accounted for. Who is missing?"

"Simon; we think he went to stay with some relatives who live nearby." As if on cue, there was another knock on the door Thomas had closed as soon as Joseph and his party were through the door.

"Is anyone in there? It's me, Simon." Peter recognized the voice then nodded to Thomas, who opened the door and let in the "missing member" of their group. "Peace to all here. Peter!" Simon rushed over to his friend and grabbed his arms and then looked around. "Are you all—are we all safe?" He too started to count the faces of the men and realized that two were missing. "Who is not here, Peter?"

41

"John is with Mary at Joseph's house." Peter nodded to Joseph as Simon turned to look at and nod to the older man. "Judas is dead. He killed himself."

"No! Why, Peter?"

"Because he betrayed our master!" Nathaniel said from the back of the room. Obviously, Peter's comment from the night before about their collective guilt had not changed Nathaniel's mind about Judas.

After just staring at Nathaniel, Peter turned back to Simon and said softly, "We don't know why he killed himself, Simon. It could have been grief. It could have been remorse. It could have been any of a number of reasons why. All we do know is that he too is dead."

Simon shook his head in disbelief and started to say something, but Peter put up his hand in a motion to stop him.

"Did you see any patrols, hear any news about whether the authorities are looking for us as you made your way here, Simon?" The other man shook his head.

"No, Peter, all is quiet on the streets. No pronouncements. No extra patrols that I could see. It's just another day in Jerusalem."

Peter looked at the floor. "Yes, another day, another day in Jerusalem," was all he said as he turned and walked back over to the table where he had spent the night, sat down, and once more began to stare at the cup that sat on the table.

Joseph watched the other men hang their heads as well and start to move away from the middle of the room, where they'd all been standing. "Well," he said to no one in particular, "my servants will clean up the room. You are welcome to stay here as long as you like. Here." He pointed to packages the servants had brought in and placed on the main table in the room. "Here is food and drink. I suspect you all must be hungry." His comments seemed to awaken their stomachs as all but Peter eagerly moved toward the food and began to go through the parcels, pick out some bread, fruit, and meat, and then pour themselves a drink from one of the three jars on the table—two containing water, while one contained a common wine. Joseph saw Peter sitting by himself off to the side, then he walked over and sat down beside him.

"Not hungry, Peter?" Peter didn't look up from staring at the cup in his hands.

"No, thank you, Joseph, but I have no appetite today."

"Well, I can understand that, given the events of yesterday." Joseph shook his head. "Tragic, simply tragic." For some reason, Peter looked up at Joseph.

"What do you mean by that?"

"I mean everything that led up to Jesus's death. It shouldn't have happened. He should still be alive, here with you, with us."

Peter was confused and tired. "I'm sorry, Joseph, but I am not following you."

"I just mean things seemed to get out of hand in the Sanhedrin. Jesus was no threat to them—to us," he corrected as he realized he was still part of that body regardless of how he now felt about its other members. "But some of them, they saw him as a threat to their positions, to their power. His message certainly did

43

not call for anyone to have to go through them to get to God.

"But it never should have gotten to the point it did. To where they took him to the Romans." He spit on the floor. "A curse on them for the scum they are. It should have been taken care of within our own offices, not turn him over to the cursed Romans on some pretext that he was a threat to Rome.

"And then for all to yell and scream for that real criminal, Barabbas, and for Pilate to release him to the crowd instead of Jesus. I mean…" Joseph looked at Peter and put his hand on Peter's arm. A much easier task this time as both men were seated. "You were there, Peter." Peter shot a glance at Joseph and then cast his eyes down again without saying anything.

"You saw it, didn't you? You were there at the trial and again at the cross. Tell me, what did you see? What did Jesus say? I was not there because after I saw where things were headed, I waited at Pilate's office to at least get Jesus's body released to me rather than it just being thrown in a common grave like the others the Romans crucify." Joseph turned to face Peter. "Tell, me, please, Peter. What did you see?"

Peter never looked up as he responded, "I-I was not there, Joseph. I saw nothing. I heard nothing. I was not there."

Joseph was stunned. "You weren't there? Where were you then? You were his closest friend, Peter. I know it. I saw the way he looked at you, the way he talked to you. You should have been there! Where were you?" Tears were now falling from Peter's eyes. Joseph didn't notice them until Peter spoke again.

"I was not there, Joseph. I was not there."

Joseph was still incredulous, but he knew he was going to get no more details from the other man, so he stopped the line of questioning. He assumed Peter had a good reason for not being at the cross, and he also assumed Peter was crying for love at the loss of his dead friend. Both assumptions were wrong, but Joseph shrugged and stood up. "Excuse me, my friend. I need to see how the servants are doing taking care of the room and the others." And he walked off, calling to his servants to give him a report on their progress.

SEVEN

Mary Magdalene waited until it was light, and then she started walking toward Jesus's tomb. As she got near, she could see the guards were still there. It was a new group, not the same ones from the evening before. She made sure she could not be seen by them and then stopped and stood by a low-slung stone wall that separated her from the garden where the tomb was located. She had hoped to get close to the tomb, perhaps to even see if she could somehow move the stone and thus be able to come back later in the day to anoint the body of Jesus. But she had not foreseen the continued presence of the guards and now was at a loss as to what to do.

She looked around and saw that if she went to her left, there was a small rise from which she could look down on the tomb; and there was sufficient shrubbery to ensure that, if she sat on the ground, she probably would not be seen by the guards. She quietly made her way to this position and sat there, looking at the tomb and thinking about her lost friend. How much he had done for her with only a look and a few kind words. How he had turned her life around.

As she sat there, the temptation to return to her old ways of "earning friends" crept into her mind. Then she looked at the tomb and remembered what Jesus had said about "forgiving them for they know not what they do," or similar words, as he hung on the cross. She realized if, in that moment of pain and loss, he could, stay true to his message and perspective, she could do the same as well. Instantly, she felt a rush within her which, despite her grief at Jesus's loss, gave her a sense of calm and contentment the likes of which she'd not felt since the day Jesus had saved her from being stoned. It was almost as if he was standing beside her again, giving her the strength to choose to change and stay in the course that change entailed. The feeling was so strong she looked around, quickly thinking she might see Jesus, yet she was alone.

Am I alone? she asked herself. *I feel like he is here with me, helping me make the right choices as he did just a few months ago.* Then she looked at the tomb again. "But that is where he is now, there inside that tomb" she muttered. Despite the evidence before her—the tomb where she had seen Jesus's body placed the day before, the guards she'd seen right after the tomb was sealed, and the ones who were there now, providing evidence his body must still be in the tomb—she still felt something else was going on in regards to Jesus. Somehow, she could not bring herself to fully accept the fact that this, this cave with the large stone and the guards, was the end of it all. She didn't know how to express her thoughts, even to herself, but she felt them nevertheless. Something else was at play; she just could not express what that something was.

EIGHT

Mary had spent a restless night as the horrors of her son's crucifixion kept replaying in her mind along with memories of all the kind and gentle things he'd done for others throughout his life and all the different experiences she had encountered from prior to his birth through his early years. All of them tumbled and jumbled in her mind, making for a fitful night during which she got very little sleep. She rubbed her eyes, still very red and puffy from crying, and stretched to try and wring some small amount of rest from the bed. As she rolled over to her right, her view changed from the interior wall of the room to the ceiling and then to the small window that was high in the right wall of the room as viewed from the door.

Her bed was more or less in the center of the room, with a small table on each side. The table on the right side of the bed now bore a small tray with a jug of water, some bread, and some fruit. As she sat up, she realized that she was quite hungry, recalling how she'd not had any sort of food since early yesterday. It was then she had been called from her cousin's house in Jerusalem by one of Jesus's followers with the news that he'd been condemned to death by Pilate and was even then walking toward the place of execution. Biting into the bread and the fruit, she recalled how she had hurried along the side streets that paralleled the route on which Jesus was being led, and had met her son— only briefly—as he made his way toward Golgotha, where most of the more public executions were carried out by the Romans. They had said nothing to each other. He had obviously been beaten in some manner or other, and she had noticed right away the crown of thorns that had been driven into his scalp. For some reason, she now wondered what had happened to that item as she recalled it had been removed when she had her last look at his body in the tomb.

The food restored her spirits a bit; at least she was no longer hungry along with everything else that weighed on her heart. She also wanted to freshen up as she had gone to bed in the clothes she'd worn the day before. As if anticipating her needs, someone had laid out towels, a large basin of water, and fresh clothes for Mary. *Blue*, she thought to herself, *my favorite color*. It struck her as an odd thought to have at this moment, but then she also thought maybe there is only so much sorrow and grief a heart can take until it decides it has to focus on some other less-weighty topics just to keep on beating.

An hour or so later, Mary walked in to the main part of Joseph's house. Immediately, two of his servants approached her, bowed, and asked if there was anything she needed. She smiled, thanked them, and shook her head no. She then walked out in to the central garden around which the house had been built. It was not quite midmorning, and the air was still fresh from the rains of yesterday and the cooling winds of the night before. She found John sitting in the garden deep in contemplation. She was standing next to him before he realized she was there. Somewhat startled by her seemingly sudden appearance, he stood to greet her.

"Good morning to you, Mary. How are you feeling?"

Mary smiled and took John's hand. "As well as can be expected, John. As well as can be expected."

"Did you sleep? Are you hungry? Do you need anything?" It was apparent his concern was heartfelt and genuine. Again, the older woman smiled at the man who was so much like her son in so many ways.

"I got some rest, and having had the chance to wash up and change into some fresh clothes was very refreshing. Plus, someone had also put food in my room, and that satisfied my hunger just fine." John looked puzzled as, to the best of his recollection, no one had entered her room all night. He had purposefully put himself in the position to watch her door to ensure she would not be disturbed.

Maybe I dozed off, and one of the servants saw to her needs early this morning, John thought to himself, trying to determine how the food and clothes had gotten into Mary's room. It was not something to worry her with, however, so he kept his thoughts to himself. Mary was speaking again.

"It's nice and cool this morning." She looked up at the cloudless sky. "The storm yesterday seems to have cleared all the dust out of the air."

John looked up too. "Yes, it does." He looked at Mary again. "Do you need anything, Mary?" He paused.

"I hope you don't mind me calling you Mary. I'm not sure that I can get used to calling you Mother. I mean I think it will take some time." Again, there was that sweet and cheering smile from Mary.

No matter how bad things ever were, John thought to himself, *her smile always makes the bleakest situation look better. It just seems to give you the hope and the determination to go on regardless.*

"Mary is just fine, John, if that makes you more comfortable." She patted his arm. "Don't worry. I'll be fine, but I do appreciate your caring for me nevertheless."

"It's the least I can do, given all you and your son have done for us." John looked down and shook his head. Then he looked at Mary, whose expression now seemed to show some discomfort, something which made John sad, having referred to Jesus. "I'm sorry if my comment caused you any pain, Mary." She looked up and vigorously shook her head no. John turned a bit and looked up at the clear sky. "I still can't believe he is gone, and yet…" He turned to face her. "And yet, I also can't help but feel that—I don't know—what we saw yesterday just isn't the end. That there is something else, there is more to happen. All that he said, all that he did, it just doesn't seem possible all those good things can end with yesterday." Mary smiled. It was a smile of sincerity, but one tinged with exhaustion.

"I have been thinking those same things, John. I feel—I believe there is a message in all he said that we just cannot yet understand or decipher. I am sure he talked to you and the other eleven about this. Knowing my son, I suspect he shared with you some glimpses of what was going to happen—what did happen yesterday. I never expected him to become a great king or a great leader of men as we Jews tend to look upon those whom we would call 'great leaders' from our heritage, like David or Solomon or Joshua.

"But I knew he could lead men and women in a different way." She closed her eyes and moved her hands together and brought them up to just below her lips. "I can almost see in my mind's eye what that way was or is to be. But it is as if a curtain is keeping me from seeing it clearly." She looked up at John. "I know it is there, and it is yet to be, John. His different way is yet to be. We will just have to wait and see what is revealed to us." John nodded his agreement. Once again, Mary smiled at the young man and put her hands on his shoulders.

"Now, I really do not wish to be seen or to go anywhere today, John. My feelings are too confused, and I am afraid they might be misread by anyone coming to visit me or if I were to go to someone else's house to be consoled. However, I would like to know that Jesus's other friends are unharmed. I suspect they are at the same room where you had the Passover seder with Jesus, in the place Joseph, our host, owns. If you wouldn't mind, I would like to know that they are all right as well."

"Are you sure you will be all right here by yourself?"

Mary smiled. "Yes, John. I'll be fine. Only a few people know where I am, and the servants will take care of me just as they did earlier with the food and clothing. Now, please go. Bring my love to all of them, and come back and tell me they are all well."

John squeezed her hands, knowing any further debate with this small but determined woman would be pointless. He smiled at her, nodded, and turned and walked to the main hall of the house where his cloak was. One of the servants saw John get his cloak and immediately hastened to open the door for him. Mary watched as John spoke to the servant who glanced in her direction and nodded in affirmation of whatever John had told him. Then he was out the door.

The servant looked at Mary, smiled slightly, bowed, and went back to his chores as Mary settled on one of the cushions covering the stone seats scattered throughout the garden. She looked up at the sky again, sighed and shook her head as some tears welled in her eyes, and then just looked toward the ground and silently prayed.

Gaius the centurion had also spent a restless night. The large amount of wine he had drunk, even the success he had at the dice game, had not driven the image of that woman's face from his mind. He kept reliving, hearing actually, the voice of Jesus asking his father to forgive them "for they know not what they do." And seeing the eyes of that woman, saying the same thing to him with her eyes, not accusing him but rather asking him, "Do you realize what you have just done? Who you have killed?" But there were no answers, just the questions and the sleeplessness from looking for answers.

He was not scheduled for duty this day, so he decided to go out and walk in the city to see if there might be answers in the streets and from the people he would meet. The combination of his strong physique and Roman manner of dressing got him more than a few glances and caused almost all he encountered to veer away from him. Judeans wanted nothing to do with a Roman—any Roman.

It suddenly occurred to him if someone did approach him, it might be to assassinate him, not because he had killed their friend yesterday, but just because he was a Roman. Yet the further he walked, the less concern he had about his safety. It was almost as if he first had to find the answers to the questions racing and replaying in his mind. "Do you realize what you have just done? Do you know who you have killed?"

He stopped and shook his head. No, he did not know who he had supervised the killing of, yesterday. No, he did not realize if anything other than a simple execution of an enemy of Rome had taken place under his command. However, he now felt the answer was near, literally close to him. He looked around. He was in one of the nicer residential areas of Jerusalem, where the leading citizens lived, were catered to, and were cared for by armies of servants, similar to the way in which the patrician class in Rome was treated. One house in particular seemed to command his attention, although he did not know why. It was across the street, and he could see the tops of trees that must make up a garden behind the high, whitewashed wall. A man in the uniform of a temple guard was heading toward him, eyeing him suspiciously. Gaius tried to look as unthreatening as possible as he greeted the other man.

"Excuse me, friend. I am looking for the house of an acquaintance, but I am new to this part of the city. Can you tell me who lives in that house over there?" he said as he pointed to the place that held his interest.

The guard was even more wary now as the man's story was clearly a lie. No Roman would have friends in this part of Jerusalem. Yet for some reason, he felt he owed the man an answer. So as soon as he walked away, he would forget why he had told the Roman stranger that the house he was looking at belonged to Joseph of Arimithea.

Gaius's face brightened as he recalled the name as belonging to the man who had been given permission to bury Jesus. He turned to thank the man for his reply, but he was nowhere to be seen. Gaius was alone in the street, still wondering what the answers might be to the questions tormenting him but sensing those answers might be within the walls of that house.

NINE

Joseph was well satisfied with the work his servants had done in cleaning the room and laying out the food and drink for Jesus's apostles. Focused on supervising their work, he had forgotten about his earlier conversation with Peter until he looked over at the solitary figure still seated at the side table, still focused on the cup in his hands. *It's almost as if that cup gives him some sort of—I don't know—peace of mind or security*, Joseph thought to himself. *I still do not understand his earlier comments. What does he mean 'he wasn't there'? Perhaps it is just too painful for him to remember now. Oh well, I must be going, so I will extend to Peter my farewell.*

He walked over to Peter, who looked up when he sensed Joseph's approach and stood to greet him. Peter seemed a little less distant now. "Thank you, Joseph, for your kindness today and yesterday. I recall now how you mentioned earlier not being at his death..." Peter's voice trailed off, and then like a sail filling as it captured a passing breeze, he found his voice again. "That you were not at his crucifixion because you were with the Romans. Thank you for taking care of Jesus's burial." Peter looked around at his colleagues scattered throughout the room; some by themselves, others talking quietly together. "That task should have fallen to us, but we were scared. Scared of our own people. Scared of the Romans." Peter shook his head and put his hand on the older man's shoulder. "You showed more courage than we did, my friend."

Joseph clasped Peter's arm. "I was not threatened like you, Peter. I was part of the group which turned him over to the Romans. I am ashamed to admit it, but it was some of my colleagues who argued, for many wrong reasons I believe, Jesus was a threat to Rome, and therefore, he had to be eliminated. The Romans, scum that they are, used Jesus to foster their own reign of terror, not to satiate a few old men like myself.

"Thus for me, it is a doubly sad day. I too lost a good friend yesterday, and I lost respect for my fellow members of the Sanhedrin as well. I think I shall not be able to sit with them again. The shame and the anger I feel, despite what Jesus told us about loving our neighbors, it is just too great for me to ignore."

Joseph looked down at the cup Peter still held. "I notice, Peter, you seem to be fascinated with this cup," he said as he pointed to it. Peter looked at the cup as well, almost as if he was wondering how it had gotten into his hands.

"Yes, this is the cup Jesus used during our seder the day before yesterday. It is strange, but it comforts me to hold it. In a way, it is as if I am touching Jesus when it is in my hands." Peter looked directly at Joseph, who now saw something in Peter's eyes that had not been there before. It was a mixture of determination, faith, and remembrance. Peter's voice was different, almost reverential, when he next spoke. "Jesus said something very interesting, Joseph, very meaningful, very—what is the word—yes, profound as he held this cup. He called it a new covenant, a covenant of his blood, shed for many for their redemption. He also told us to do likewise and to remember him when we did."

"Do what 'likewise,' Peter?"

"I'm not quite sure, Joseph, but I believe he wants us to remember him and what he did for us, how he… died, yes, how he died for us whenever…" Peter looked around the room and noticed how all the other men had stopped talking. Those closest to him were listening intently to him; the others were moving toward him to ensure they could hear what he had to say.

Peter nodded. "Yes, I think he wants us to remember him whenever we gather as a group for a meal. Remember what he did for us, for what he stood, and what he said. And we shall do that, shall we not, my friends?" The other all murmured their agreement, many of them secretly rejoicing that the Peter they knew from before, the born leader, had once again assumed the mantle of leadership. It raised their spirits tremendously.

Joseph could feel the change in the mood, and he too was buoyed by Peter's comments. He turned and looked at the cup, then at Peter. "Peter, I believe this cup you hold is very special. I also believe, for reasons I cannot explain, that you are to be a person who will neither have, nor care about material possessions in your life. I believe this cup should be safeguarded and preserved, and I have the wherewithal to do just that.

May I take it and keep it safe for you and for all of these other friends of Jesus?" he said as he swept his arm around the room.

"Yes, Joseph. I think you are right." Peter carefully handed him the cup. "I have one favor to ask though."

"Anything my friend," Joseph said as he carefully wrapped the cup in a clean towel he had been carrying.

"Whenever I, or any of my friends here visit with you, you will allow us a few moments with this cup. Keep it safe for all of us, Joseph."

"My home is your home, Peter, yours and all of these others. I will be honored and blessed to have you visit and dwell under my roof, if even for a brief time. And I promise you, this cup will be there for you." He looked at the others. "For all of you. This I promise."

"Thank you, Joseph." Peter looked up as there was a knock on the door. Thomas ran to his self-appointed gatekeeper post and challenged the visitor.

"It is I, John."

"Are you alone?" Thomas asked, not thinking it was possible John was being threatened by others outside the door to say he was by himself.

"Yes, I am alone, Thomas." The sincerity of the reply was enough for Thomas, who unbolted the door then, once again, positioned himself to force it closed just in case, and the other man entered by himself. John saw the others standing close to Peter and immediately made his way to his friend.

"Peace to you, Peter, and to all of you," he said as he acknowledged his fellow apostles, and they, some of them smiling for the first time in two days, returned his salutation.

Joseph looked over John's shoulder. "Where is Mary, John? Who is with her?"

"She is safe and well at your house, Joseph. I spoke with your head servant before I left. She will be fine. She insisted I come here to bring you her greeting and to return with news of everyone's well-being."

Peter smiled. "That is good news, John. Joseph, we are even more indebted to you than before. Thank you for taking care of Mary."

Joseph looked embarrassed. "Peter, it is I who am blessed and thankful I can do such a thing for such a great lady. But I do not want to leave her alone for too long. So with your permission, I will take my leave of you. My servants will return later today with more food and drink." Joseph looked somewhat severely at Peter. "I doubt you, Peter, or any of you are in any real threat. But I suggest you stay here at least for one more day as, if nothing else, there will be more people in the streets tomorrow. It will also give me more time to find out what is the situation in regards to Jesus's followers. But if anyone *is* looking for you, tomorrow you will be harder to find because of the crowds." Joseph bowed. "Peace to all of you."

"And to you, Joseph. Thank you again," Peter replied as the others murmured their assent as well. Joseph and his servants were let out by Thomas, who added his own thanks as the trio exited the room. Now it was just the eleven.

Peter looked at the door for a few moments. Then he looked around at his fellow followers of Jesus. All was silent. All were looking at him. He put his head down for a short period of time and then looked up, knowing they were looking for encouragement and strength from him.

"My friends, my brothers," he began, "I agree with Joseph's recommendation we stay here for at least one more day. But it is not because I am any longer worried about my safety. I have been doing much thinking, recalling what our Master said to us over the last couple of years. Some of it was easy to understand, such as instructing us to love one another and to love our neighbors.

"But, quite honestly, much of what he said is still hard for me to understand. His frequent comments over the last several weeks about destroying the temple and raising it up again. Or his comments about how one had to die to live again." He looked at the others and smiled slightly.

"I must be honest with you my friends. I am very confused by those comments, and I suspect you are as well." All nodded their heads in agreement. "But I also keep coming back to one thing. It is something hard for me to put into words, but I will try. I keep thinking that what happened yesterday just cannot be the end. It just does not make sense if you think about all Jesus said and did. It would be like…like if we went to our boats, cleaned and fixed out nets, loaded them on to the boats, rowed out in to the middle of the water, and then just sat there." Peter shook his head. "Everything he did, everything he said, to me, they all point to something else, something other than him being executed by the Romans as a common criminal. I think something else is going to happen." Peter pointed to the floor. "And as this was the last place where we were all together with him, I think we should be *here* when it happens."

"When what happens?" Thomas asked. Peter looked at the other man and shook his head.

"I don't know, Thomas. I'm sorry. It is more of a feeling than anything. But I can tell you it is a very strong feeling, like…like Jesus is still with us in something other than our memories. And that he wants us to stay here, and to stay together, at least for a day or two more." John moved toward Peter, placing himself in the center of the group.

"It's interesting you say that, Peter. I was talking with Mary earlier today. She is sad as you would expect. Yet she too seems to have some feelings of hope or a feeling something is going to happen" he said as he looked at the group. Then he turned to Peter. "It is very much as you described it, Peter, very much the same. With your permission, I am going to go back and check on her, and then I will return."

"Go in peace, my friend, and bring Mary our love."

"I will. Peace to all of you." The rest returned John's greeting, and Thomas saw him to and through the door. He too, like all of the men in the room, had some sense of events yet to come, but he still had his concerns about the Romans and the temple guard. So he made sure to lock and bar the door following John's departure.

Peter moved toward the table where Joseph's servants had left the food and drink. He suddenly realized how very hungry he was as he had eaten nothing since Thursday night's seder. He filled a plate with bread, meat, and fruit, poured some wine into a cup, and moved away from the table so the others who had all lined up behind him could also get something to eat.

All ate in silence, each man lost in his thoughts, memories, and questions about what had happened and what might yet come to be. When they had finished and cleaned up their plates—they were their own servants now—they all returned and sat close to Peter. They each drew courage from the big man and, in doing so, helped him realize he had to show strength and put his own shame and worries to the side for now.

"My friends, now that our stomachs aren't making so much noise grumbling at each other"—his comment brought a smile to all—"I think we should spend some time in prayer. Let us recall the psalms David left us, and let us all, each on our own, also recall the words our Master spoke to us." He paused for a second. "Each of us should think and recall those words Jesus spoke, which bring you strength, peace, and comfort to watch and wait." His face brightened as he recalled one of Jesus's parables. "Remember Jesus's story about the bridesmaids waiting for the bridegroom?" All of the men shook their heads as they recalled the story. "I think that is us now, waiting to see what happens. While it is day, we are not waiting through the night. But it is as if we are in the dark for now. We cannot see what is coming, but I believe we all know. We all believe yesterday was not the end.

"Everything Jesus told us spoke of a new order, a-a new world as it were. That will not be possible if yesterday's events are 'the end.'" Peter shook his head slowly as he looked at the floor and then at his companions. "No, that would just not be right. It would be as if, well, for those of us who are fisherman, it would be as if we spent all night mending our nets and tending to our boats, and when the sun came up, we saw the lake was gone, disappeared. All that preparation, all that work, and then nowhere to ply our trade.

"No, something else is going to happen. I am sure Jesus, in speaking to us, told us what it was to be. But I must confess that right now, my friends, I cannot recall what those words were, or I cannot understand them even though I am sure he told us what to expect.

"So now, each of you pray to our God. Pray for strength. Pray for faith. Pray for each other." With that, Peter stood up and walked over to the table where he had spent much of the past day and a half. This time though, he turned his chair so it was facing the middle of the room, ensuring all could see him. He wasn't trying to make himself the center of attention; he realized the needs and fears of each man in the room were different. And if just by seeing Peter could help one of them, then that was all the motivation he needed to be available to them, if only by a glance.

While the conversation had brightened Peter's mood somewhat, it darkened again as he recalled Jesus's words. His thoughts immediately went to the times when Jesus had spoken about forgiving the hurt another had done to you as well as seeking their forgiveness from wrongs you had done to them. He shuddered involuntarily as his memories returned to the night before last, after Jesus had been taken by the guards. Peter just started following them; he had no plan as to what he was going to do. He surely could not have "rescued" Jesus; he was outnumbered by at least thirty to one. He just felt that he needed to be near Jesus.

Peter was impetuous, and it was this personality trait that, if nothing else, compelled him to walk right in to the courtyard of the chief priest's quarters. It was there that the situation really started going from bad to worse for the fisherman from Galilee. First, it was the others sitting by the fire who questioned his accent. Then it was the servant girl who swore she recognized him as one of Jesus's followers. He now recalled how he got more and more nervous; he began to feel trapped, sensing the walls as well as the crowd, were closing in on him. He shuddered again as he recalled seeing the guards take notice of the commotion and starting to move toward it.

Then there was another accusation about being a follower of Jesus hurled at him. He had stood up and, focused solely on his own survival, lashed out with curse-laced denials that he knew Jesus. He had sworn that he had never followed him; that he had no interest in whoever this person was.

Peter recalled that as he spoke, he had also slowly moved toward the gate; the ferocity of his swearing and walking away his only defense. He had been somewhat relieved when no one moved to intercept him nor really pay any more attention to him once he was in the shadows at the edge of the fire's glow.

As he had turned to walk through the gate and to freedom, however, another light caught his eye: the first glow of dawn. With that first glow, Peter suddenly heard a cock crowing in the distance. Just as suddenly, he recalled the prophetic words of Jesus concerning Peter's denial of him, and he had collapsed against the outer wall of the courtyard, trying to hold back the sobs but failing; just as he had failed his friend a few moments earlier.

Bitterly remembering his betrayal of his friend, he wondered if Jesus could ever forgive him or if he could ever forgive himself; and once more, he began to cry. The others noticed it and were troubled by this display of emotion, which they incorrectly interpreted as some sort of fear or despair about his and their future.

Peter sensed he was once again the center of attention and wiped his eyes as he looked up and saw all eyes fixed on him. "Forgive me, my friends. I do not weep out of fear or despair but for...for...for personal reasons. I weep for my own, for my lack of courage when our Master needed it most. Forgive my tears. I am looking back when I should be looking ahead."

This time it was Andrew, Peter's brother, who spoke up. "My brother, I know you better than all of these our friends. I know not of what betrayal you speak, but now we are all with you in feeling sad about our recent lack of courage. Do not think you bear that sorrow and shame alone." Andrew looked around the room at the others. "We all bear it with you, Peter. We all do." The others nodded their affirmation of Andrew's comments. Peter could only shake his own head and smile wanly as he touched his brother's cloak as if to say thank you.

Each man resumed his solitary thoughts and prayers. At first, Peter's thoughts again turned to Jesus's teaching about forgiving others. Then Peter had a thought; he was clearly sorry for what he had done. He knew if he could somehow go back in time, he would not make the same mistake again. Even though he knew Jesus was dead, in his heart Peter asked Jesus to forgive him. Suddenly, he thought he heard a voice, one as strong and as clear as if the person speaking was standing next to him. Yet as he looked around, he was alone; the nearest person was at least six feet away. He shook his head and closed his eyes; and again, he heard the voice, only this time he recognized it. It was Jesus telling him as he had only a few weeks earlier, "Thou art Peter, and upon this rock I will build my church; and the gates of hell shall not prevail against it."[6]

When he opened his eyes, Peter saw he was still alone, or was he? For he felt a presence and a peace of mind, which had alluded him for the last day and a half. He realized he was no longer alone, and while he might never forget his betrayal of his friend, somebody else already had, and that someone had other plans for this former fisherman.

TEN

Phineas, the Levite, walked into the chambers of the Sanhedrin following Sabbath prayers. As he expected, Caiaphas, the current high priest was sitting there, reading from a scroll. "Peace to you, Caiaphas." The older man looked up.

"Ah, Phineas, peace to you as well. How are you this fine day, my friend?" Phineas sat down heavily next to Caiaphas.

"I am troubled, Caiaphas, about this 'Jesus' matter. I did not sleep well last night as I kept thinking about it."

Caiaphas carefully rolled up the scroll, nodded, and handed it to a scribe, who walked away, recognizing the nod from the high priest as a signal he wished to be alone with the other man. He turned to face Phineas.

"Of what are you troubled, Phineas? That a traitor to Rome was discovered and given the proper sentence due any such traitor?"

"No, Caiaphas. I am troubled over our role in that death. How we decided, how we turned him over to the Romans. One of our own, Caiaphas, a fellow Jew." Caiaphas shook his head.

"No, he may have been Jewish by birth, but he was not one of us. Listen, Phineas. You know that we, the Sanhedrin, are the only true authority our people have. It is not the Romans, a curse be upon them, or Herod, the feckless fool of a Roman puppet. It is us, the Sanhedrin. We are the ones who provide real authority and real guidance to our people. We are the keepers and guardians of our faith, our traditions. Do you not agree?" The other man nodded his head.

"Then you understand we must carefully maintain and preserve our authority. Part of that authority means we must be the intermediaries with the likes of Pilate and Herod. We must be looked up to by them, treated as equals, even though they are beneath us.

"Look at all the trouble of a year or so ago with that wild man, John, who had been preaching and baptizing people in the Jordan. Look what happened when he challenged Herod. Do you remember all the trouble we had, dealing with Herod for months after he had John killed? The situation came very close to being disastrous as I now know Pilate was getting very upset with Herod's inability to function. Think what would have happened. Think what we would have lost if Pilate had established real martial law over all of Judea.

"So along comes this son of a carpenter from Nazareth, making wild claims, doing magic tricks, and once again upsetting the supposed rulers of Judea—Herod and Pilate. He was a threat to our country. He was a threat to the established authority, both their and ours. It was our duty to uncover him and turn him over to the Romans before he caused any real trouble.

"I mean look at how people were flocking to him. Why? Because he supposedly fed a number of them once or twice. Because he did tricks, which confused and amused them. It was only a matter of time until Pilate would have used him as an excuse to come down hard on all of us. So we had to do it for the good of our people and our faith." Phineas looked hard at the other man.

"Do you really believe what you just said, Caiaphas? Do you really? I mean what harm did the man do? Everything I've heard about him is whatever tricks or deeds he did never hurt anyone, but rather, all he did seemed to be for the benefit of people."

Caiaphas looked down and shook his head. "Phineas, have you heard what the Romans do in Rome? They have these big festivals where they give the people free food and have spectacles and fights between animals, sometimes between fighting men and the animals. All for 'the people.' Do they do this because they want the people to be happy, to gain some benefit? No, they do this to ensure they can maintain control over the people.

"I think that is what this Jesus was trying to do—gain control of the people for who-knows-what reason. No, my friend, as I see it, the only 'benefit' out of what he was doing was to benefit himself."

Phineas sat quietly for a few minutes. What the elder man was saying made sense. A delicate balance did need to be maintained in Judea if the Judeans were to preserve what few freedoms they still possessed, most importantly their religious freedom. Yet he still did not feel right about what the Sanhedrin had done earlier in the week. Caiaphas read the doubt in the other man's face. *We can't have doubters amongst our leaders*, he thought to himself. "Phineas let me ask you a question. How do you keep a dog happy? How do you keep it from biting you?" Phineas looked puzzled, trying to figure out the nature of the question.

"I don't know. Feed it, I guess. Give it something it likes, like a bone or something to chew on from time to time."

"Exactly, give it a bone to chew on so it doesn't chew on you or your possessions. This Jesus, believe me, he was a threat to Judea. But he was also a 'bone' we could throw to the Romans. Let them chew on him versus chewing on us and our families. I know this is a hard thing to hear, my friend, but it is the reality of the times and the world in which we live. Praise God if he wills it the Romans will leave us or be driven out by us one of these days. But in the meantime, we need to throw them a bone once in a while to keep them from chewing on us. Now do you understand?"

Phineas was even more depressed than when he had first walked in. But unfortunately, what the high priest said made sense to him. He looked at the other man who was sitting patiently, waiting for a reply. "Yes, Caiaphas, I understand. I do not like it, but I understand."

"None of us 'likes' it, Phineas, but sometimes we must do what we do not like to ensure we survive." He patted the other man on the shoulder. "Now, go, my friend, and worry about this no more. Relax and enjoy the rest of the Sabbath. Peace to you, Phineas," he said as he turned and clapped his hands, and the scribe reappeared with another scroll. Obviously, the meeting was at an end.

"Peace to you, Caiaphas. Peace to you," was all Phineas could mutter as he slowly got up and walked out of the chamber, his steps weighed down by a heart now filled with both sadness *and* regret.

ELEVEN

On his way back to his house, Joseph decided to pay a visit to Jesus's tomb. He knew it was being watched by temple guards, and owing to his position on the Sanhedrin, he also knew most of the guards would recognize him and thus would not be surprised by his being there. He stopped for a second just out of their line of sight to observe them. Three guards were on duty. One of them was sleeping under the shade of a nearby tree; the other two stood with their backs to the sleeping guard, talking. What Joseph could not know was that one of them had spotted Mary Magdalene on the hill above the tree. She had actually fallen asleep and, thus, remained where she was as the two guards conversed. With their backs to her, one of them said to the other: "Don't look up, but someone is lying on the hill above the tree. I cannot tell who it might be, but my guess is that it is one of the followers of this Jesus. I'm going to circle around and see if I can capture him; it might give us some sport, as opposed to just sitting here guarding a dead man."

As the guard started to move toward Mary, the other caught sight of Joseph's party and signaled his companion with a low whistle. Both stood in somewhat of a defensive stance as they saw Joseph approach, while simultaneously trying to rouse the third member of their party. They also forgot about the person on the hill. Initially relaxing somewhat when they recognized Joseph, fear suddenly gripped both of them. Their colleague was still asleep, and thoughts of what would happen to all of them when Joseph reported their laxness to the Sanhedrin flooded their mind.

"Hail Joseph, most worthy member of the Sanhedrin!" one of them said in a voice loud enough to be heard three towns away. It had the desired effect, though, as the third guard was awakened by the noise, stood, and looked around as he tried to shake the sleep from his body while assessing what was going on and who this visitor was. He was gripped with the same fear as his comrades when he recognized a member of the Sanhedrin now standing next to the tomb, eyeing and touching the large stone as he said something that the guard could not make out.

Joseph turned as the third man approached and saluted him. He bowed slightly as a return of the salute and then looked in the direction of where the man had come. The indentation in the tall grass where he'd been lying was still clearly to be seen, but Joseph's view was suddenly drawn to something on the small hill behind and above the tree under which the guard had been lying, both of which were closer to him than where the three guards now stood. Someone was on the hill—a woman. He thought he recognized her as someone he'd seen in the company of Jesus these last couple of weeks. However, given his failing eyesight, he could not be sure.

Remembering there might be other eyes staring in the same direction, he turned to face the guards and assumed an air of authority. "Has anyone approached the tomb?" he asked brusquely. The voice startled the guards and focused their attention on him.

Meanwhile, Joseph's servants tried very hard to keep from laughing as they recognized the voice Joseph used when a new slave or servant was introduced to the household. They called it the "lion's roar," but as they both knew from experience it was an act on Joseph's part. In reality, he was the epitome of a gentle soul. But it could be a convincing act, nevertheless, as they now witnessed it grab and hold the attention of the three guards who were all answering simultaneously, enthusiastically trying to convince Joseph of their keen watchfulness. Joseph harrumphed just to drive home the necessity of them staying alert as well as to ensure that if they had seen anyone on the hill, it was now the furthest thing from their mind.

Satisfied that he had sufficiently displayed his authority and made sure any report back to the Sanhedrin would speak of his diligence in supporting the guards' duties, Joseph nodded to the trio, turned quickly, and started walking off to the left. His servants followed closely behind, still trying to restrain themselves, particularly as they noticed the growing wet spot on the pants of the guard who had been sleeping. If the three had several more hours on duty, they were going to be uncomfortable ones for both him and his companions.

When they were out of earshot of the guards, Joseph motioned for one of his servants to walk beside him as he instructed the servant to go back to the hill and make a show of double-checking the guards while finding out who was hiding under the lip of the hill. Joseph told the servant if he recognized the person, he was to bring the person back with him. The servant nodded, turned, and headed back the short distance to the hill. There he found Mary Magdalene, who had fallen asleep several hours earlier, from exhaustion and the heat of the day. She had been awakened by the guards' greeting to Joseph and had popped up momentarily to see what was going on before resuming a more-hidden posture. It was during that brief time Joseph had spotted her. She had recognized him as a man of influence, although she did not know from where or what organization. She was frightened when his servant approached but followed his instruction to lie still for a few moments while he made a show of checking the guards.

The ruse worked: they saw him, saluted, and went to patrolling the tomb area, giving him enough time to have Mary creep away from the hill until he knew she could no longer be seen from the tomb. He then extended his hand to help her up and pointed in the direction of Joseph and the other servant, who were now a couple of hundred yards away. Joseph turned to see the two approaching and then looked around to see if anyone else whom he recognized was in the area;

there was none. This was not an area where members of the Sanhedrin were likely to walk, particularly on the Sabbath.

As she drew closer, Joseph recognized her as Mary Magdalene. At first, he was inclined to just dismiss her with a stern warning about staying away from the tomb. Then he remembered how she had come to a dinner where Jesus was the guest of honor and he had been present, supposedly as a "spy" for the Sanhedrin, but, in reality, to absorb more of the Master's teachings. Mary had come in and anointed Jesus's feet and dried them with her hair. It had caused quite a stir, but he now recalled how Jesus had gently but firmly reprimanded those who had grumbled about her actions and how, from that time on, she had been one of his followers. The recollection immediately softened what had been a scowl into a face in which Mary saw kindness and, more, a kindred spirit. She now recognized him as the man who had supervised the burial of Jesus. When she stood in front of him, he addressed her. "It's 'Mary', is it not?"

"It is, sir. Please forgive me."

"Forgive you for what, Mary?"

"Why, why for whatever it is I did that has caused you to summon me, sir." Joseph smiled.

"You did nothing wrong, Mary. But it is not safe for you to stay at the tomb." He looked around and waved his hand. "This is an isolated and desolate area. You could have been attacked by one of the packs of stray dogs roaming this area." He pointed back at the tomb. "Or you could have been discovered and hurt or arrested by the guards on the tomb." Mary looked down, reminding Joseph of a chastised child. Then she looked up at him again with an almost breathtaking passion in her face.

"I know that, sir, but it allowed me to be close to Jesus. To help me feel less like he is gone. For that feeling, I would risk my life." Then she remembered Joseph's actions on Friday evening, and she impulsively touched the sleeve of his cloak. "I must thank you, sir, for burying Jesus. I know you are a man of influence in this city, but I know there had to be danger for you in doing such a thing, and I want to thank you for what you did."

Joseph nodded in acknowledgement of her gratitude, making sure out of habit, however, not to touch her. He had already seen the look of horror on the faces of his servants as they watched a woman whom they had seen once or twice, but knew by "reputation," touch their beloved master. He did not want to further confuse them.

"It was the very least I could do for the Master, Mary." Mary looked up and smiled as she realized Joseph must be a believer in Jesus as well. But the quick sideway glance Joseph gave toward his servants was enough of a clue for her to say nothing more and simply nod.

"Sir, do you know what happened to his mother?"

"Yes, she is staying at my house. I know you were a follower of Jesus, Mary. Please come back with us to my home. I think Mary would be cheered by seeing you." Mary Magdalene stepped back a pace or two with a look of astonishment on her face at such a gesture from a man of authority. It was matched by the look on Joseph's servants, but their looks changed quickly when he scowled at them.

"I-I can't, sir. I-I…I am not suitably dressed to meet her."

Joseph smiled. "I've known Mary for many years, young lady. I don't think she will have the least concern about how you are dressed. Come. The visit will do you good as well, and you can join us for the Sabbath dinner." Joseph turned and started walking, clearly in no mood to further debate the invitation. Mary shook her head and fell in behind the servants, trying to brush the dust from her dress and push back her hair into place under the veil that she wore over her head.

TWELVE

It was midafternoon on the Sabbath as Pontius Pilate finished the paperwork, which was an integral part of the Roman empire's centrally managed and controlled government. He was working swiftly to get all the dispatches reviewed and signed/sealed so the courier could start his ride toward Judea's west coast. Once there, the courier would board a ship bound for Rome, and with good weather, the dispatches would be in the hands of the appropriate officials in less than two weeks' time.

As he finished reviewing and sealing the final document—the report on the trial and execution of the man called Jesus—Pilate handed the papers to his chief scribe, Septimus, with instructions he wished to be alone for a while. Septimus bowed and carried the papers out of the room to bundle them and give them to the waiting courier. Meanwhile, Pilate sat back and reflected on the papers he'd just dispatched, focusing in particular on the report of Jesus's trial and execution. He closed his eyes and recalled the words that indicated Jesus had been a subversive, identified and caught by the procurator's own agents. The report had gone on to state how there had been several witnesses to substantiate this claim, and the accused, having offered no defense, was found guilty and sentenced to death by crucifixion, the sentence having been carried out immediately after the conclusion of his trial.

Pilate remembered the accused's "defense" in particular. *The man clearly understood the seriousness of the charges against him, yet he said nothing*, Pilate thought to himself. Indeed, as he recalled the event, he again marveled at how seemingly resolved the man had been to die. Pilate was also struck by the calm manner in which the man had talked of his kingdom not being of this world and, if it had been, how his subjects would have been there fighting for his release.

Pilate shook his head. *The man was either delusional or disoriented as well as suffering from the treatment he had received at the hands of my guards. Yet I must admit some admiration for the way in which he carried himself"*, he thought. "*He had the carriage of a man of authority, and he looked me straight in the eye, nothing like all of these other Judeans who grovel and scrape in my presence. Really quite profound actually.* Pilate turned to the table at his side and poured himself a glass of wine, returning to his contemplation as he sipped the beverage.

I must admit it was somewhat uncomfortable for me to have had to disappoint my wife and her entreaties on his behalf, he thought. *But we need to make examples of Rome's subjects from time to time. And this man served that purpose. Really a bit of a shame though. It would have been interesting to have a discussion with him about topics like philosophy and life. I suspect it would have been*

81

considerably more engaging then most of the "discussions" I get to engage in with the populace here.

Pilate chuckled to himself that he had at least some sort of a conversation with this man Jesus. His spies in Herod's palace had informed him when Jesus stood before Herod, he had said absolutely nothing. Pilate was aware of Herod's interest in Jesus just as he was aware of all of Herod's other interests.

I'm sure Herod was beside himself when this Jesus just stood there silent, Pilate thought. *What a fool the man is. But like this Jesus, he serves a purpose for Rome too. For now, by living.* Pilate stood up, drained his cup, stretched a bit, and walked toward one of the openings that led from this room out onto the steps that went down to the presidium's open courtyard. He leaned against one of the columns, recalling the reaction of the mob when he brought Jesus out to the crowd. He admitted to himself it was an attempt on his part to free the man, depending upon the reaction of the crowd. *The crowd, how they turned on him.* Pilate shook his head. *What a people these Judeans are. They demand I crucify this Jesus and free a scum like Barabbas.*

He shook his head again. "What a people these Judeans are," he murmured to himself as he walked back into his office and through the door, out toward the large interior room where Septimus waited with Pilate's next appointment—a group of Jordanian tradesmen from Petra. They had been kept waiting long enough to know who was in charge in this part of the empire.

Herod had finished the ritual washings after the Sabbath meal, dismissed himself from those who had joined him for dinner, and retreated, full wine cup in hand, to his empty throne room. Like Pilate, he wanted to be alone for a while. His thoughts were not of Jesus though. They were the seething thoughts of a man who, just one night before, had been insulted and humiliated in front of his own servants by a Roman bureaucrat. It was bad enough to have to put up with any Roman, but one who clearly was a glorified bureaucrat, that was too much.

"I am a proud and honorable man, And I have to sit there and take insults and orders from a man who is probably on the lowest rung of the Roman bureaucratic ladder. If they look down on us Judeans as much as they like to say they do, how powerful can this man be? Why should I, a king, have to take any orders or insults from such a man?" he murmured to himself, conveniently forgetting how he ruled at the will of Rome and that his "kingship" could be wrested from him as easily as it had been given to his forefathers. Of course, the copious amounts of wine Herod had already consumed tended to cloud his judgment a bit as it had many times in the past.

As he wallowed in self-pity, Herod also recalled the "audience" he had granted to the man Jesus very early yesterday. *There is another one!* he thought to himself. *A carpenter's son, and he would not speak to me? Would not answer my questions! How dare he? Why I should have him arrested and see if my jailers can loosen his tongue.* Then he remembered such an act would be most difficult, owing to the fact the Romans had executed him the day before.

"Hmm...serves him right for not showing me the proper respect. The respect due to a king!" he slurred. Herod looked up as he heard the sounds of laughter and animated conversation coming from the banquet hall. He stood woozily and started weaving his way toward the noise. "That is where I belong!" he said to no one. "Amongst those who worship and adore me!" And with a sweep of his right arm, the curtain separating the two rooms was pushed aside, and Herod rejoined the party of sycophants and spies who, each for their own reasons, took pleasure in being in his company.

THIRTEEN

Mary Magdalene was thinking about the afternoon she had just spent with Joseph and Mary as she walked back to the house she was currently staying in. It was about a half hour's walk from Joseph's house, so she had plenty of time to think as she slowly walked along the streets, escorted by one of Joseph's servants. While Mary was not of noble birth or a person of stature in the community, Joseph's servants were well trained and treated anyone entrusted to their care with the same courtesy and bearing as when attending to their master and his family. Thus, even though she had a companion, Mary had been quietly left to her thoughts.

There were few people out as evening was nigh. The air had started to cool a bit as well, making it quite pleasant for those who might be walking about. However, the weather was lost on Mary. She was recalling her conversation with the other Mary following dinner. *What courage and faith the woman has*, she thought to herself. Mary could not get beyond the death of her beloved friend. His mother, however, while saddened by the death of her son, seemed to possess a belief that all was not lost, all was not at an end when it came to Jesus.

Mary Magdalene had listened intently as the other Mary talked in a low, quiet, and peaceful voice. She had tried to absorb what was being said, but she kept going back to the image of Jesus dying on the cross, of his body being carried into the tomb and the large stone being rolled across the front of it. She recalled to herself how the scene had not changed when she had visited the tomb earlier this day. And yet here was his mother, not saying anything explicit but clearly exuding calmness and a faith that Mary just could not comprehend.

Despite the strong impression Mary had made on her, Mary Magdalene found herself thinking, once again, maybe she needed to go back to her earlier ways of "making friends." She felt she was clearly missing something Jesus's mother either possessed or had said. That generated self-doubt; maybe she had missed the message behind what Jesus had said to her while he was still alive. *I can't understand this, this faith she has*, she thought to herself. *I wish I could. I wish I could possess that, but I don't think I can.*

I was treated so well by him. I should have more faith, but I do not. What have I missed? Why cannot I see what Mary can see? Why cannot I see beyond the big rock in front of his tomb? Maybe I just have to accept the fact he is gone and figure out how I go forward, how I support myself. I doubt his followers will need anything I could offer in the way of help or support. I guess I'm just on my own again.

She shuddered at that thought and was on the verge of tears when she felt someone, or something, touch her. She stopped and looked around, but there was no one within an arm's length of her. The person nearest to her was Joseph's servant, who had stopped as well, but he was at least five feet away. Yet she knew someone had just touched her; it had felt like a hand on her shoulder. Baffled yet seeing no one other than the servant, she started walking again. As she did, she once more started to contemplate how she would support herself from now on. The "old way" seemed to be her only course of action. And then she felt the touching again, this time accompanied by a quiet voice. It was as if someone was whispering in her ear. She was certain no one was standing close to her, so she slowed down her pace and focused on the voice. The message was simple. "Mary, have courage. All will reveal itself soon."

She walked a few more steps and then froze as the recognition sunk in. It was Jesus's voice. *But how is that possible?* she thought to herself. *He's dead, and I don't believe in ghosts.* Again she heard the voice. "Mary, have courage." Thoroughly confused, she walked faster toward the house where she was had been staying. At the door, she turned and thanked the servant, who bowed in response, turned, and walked away. Once inside, she went up the steps to her room, closed the door behind her, and sat on the cot, which was the only real piece of furniture in the room, save a small table that held a pitcher of water and basin for washing.

"What just happened?" she asked herself. "Am I going mad? Or am I just too tired to think clearly? Yes, that must be it. I need to rest. I can't think clearly now. I'm hearing voices, feeling like someone is touching me, not in a bad way. No, actually it felt more like support, like the hand of a friend on your shoulder when you are in need.

But there was no one there when I looked to see who was touching me! she thought to herself as she started pacing around her room. *I don't understand, and I am too tired to try and understand. I need to rest.* Once again, she said softly, "I need to rest," as she lay down on the cot and almost immediately fell into a deep and dreamless sleep.

FOURTEEN

Andrew stood up and stretched. Like the other ten men in the room, he had spent most of this day in prayer and thought, trying to make sense of what had happened and what might yet happen. His thoughts had gone back to when he had first met Jesus. He had been coming out to the Jordan River Valley to listen to the prophet John. He recalled how John was unlike any other man he had ever seen or met. He lived as a hermit in the desert, was rough-looking both in his personal appearance with long unruly hair and an unkempt beard, and his dress, wearing little more than a camel hair short tunic. But the words that he spoke, the passion with which he delivered them while still maintaining an undercurrent of humility and, yes, what could only be described as a loving kindness for those to whom the words were delivered—John was truly inspiring to Andrew.

Then one day, as John had been speaking, another man walked by, and John pointed to him, saying, "Behold the Lamb of God!7, he is the one; it is he whom you should follow." Andrew had looked at the man of whom John spoke. Without thinking, he and several others had gotten up and started walking toward the other man who turned, stopped, and looked directly at Andrew, who was now standing closest to him.

"What seek ye?"[8] the man had asked Andrew.

In reply, Andrew had exclaimed, "Where dwellest thou?"[9] He nodded as he recalled his words, suddenly realizing they had been the first ones to come to mind at that time. Yet the man's reply, something about going with him and seeing, now seemed to take on new meaning.

What was I looking for? Andrew thought to himself. *What did I see then, and what am I looking for now? Answers. I am looking for answers, but I cannot seem to find any today about Jesus, the man John pointed to that day. I am looking for answers which I cannot find.*

He shook his head and sat back down, rubbing his hands across his face, trying to wring some of the fatigue from his body. As he sat there, eyes closed and rough hands scouring his face, he felt a presence and thought he heard a voice. He opened his eyes and looked around, but no one was near him. He shook his head, sighed, and closed his eyes.

Again he heard the voice; this time, he could understand what was being said. "I am coming, and you will see the answers you seek." Startled, Andrew opened his eyes and looked around. He was still alone, but he now realized whose voice he had heard—Jesus's. His eyes grew wide with the recognition, and he scanned the room once more, searching for the Master. He was not there; only the other ten and they were all, apparently, trying to figure out what had happened and, based on several of their postures, praying for guidance as well.

He thought about saying something to his brother, Peter, but when he looked at the other man, he seemed to either be lost deep in thought or perhaps asleep.

Best to let him rest, Andrew thought. *As tired and upset as we all are, it is no wonder that I think I am hearing voices, particularly the Master's voice.* Yet he also thought the voice was not a hallucination but something real—as real as he was, sitting there in that room, wondering what might happen next.

Nathaniel, the one who had spoken out most strongly about Judas, had always been the skeptic of the group. As he sat there in the room, he too thought back to when he first heard about and then met Jesus. When informed by Philip, his friend, that they had found the Messiah, a man who had come from the town of Nazareth, Nathaniel had looked at him, shook his head, and replied, "Can there any good thing come out of Nazareth?"[10] He shook his head, regretting those words, thinking back to Philip's persistence and his reluctant following of his friend to meet this stranger. However, in their first meeting, Jesus spoke to Nathaniel with such authority and conviction that his doubts about Jesus were immediately put to rest.

Then yesterday had occurred, and the doubts and skepticism had returned. Yet as he recalled his words of yesterday and this morning, he was filled with remorse at "speaking first and thinking second." Like the others, Nathaniel was tired, scared, and confused, and he knew that he had let his emotions get the better of him. He now hoped what they had heard about Judas wasn't true, and as he looked over toward the door, he hoped the last of their band would soon walk through it and join them once more.

For his part, James was worried about his brother, John. He felt John was exposing himself to arrest and possibly execution by the Romans because he had been and was still quite visible in his association with Jesus. His standing by in the inner courtyard during Jesus's trial, his standing by Jesus's cross during his crucifixion and then taking on the role of the protector of Mary. Now John was placing himself in danger with his trips back and forth between Joseph of Arimithea's house and the room where James was sitting. *I'm worried that he's too...too exposed, putting himself in too much danger,* James thought to himself.

Then he recalled his brother's strong belief in and love for Jesus. James was emotionally close to his brother, but he knew that John was just as close to Jesus as he was to himself. He wasn't jealous; in fact, as he thought about it, he realized that John was acting and reacting just as he would if James was in peril. He thought back to the two or three times when one or the other of them had rescued his brother when his sibling had been in danger while out fishing.

He shook his head. *That is what he is doing,* James thought to himself, *taking care of his family. Well, I can't fault him for that. But I am still worried about him. So much has happened. So much is still uncertain. Not just for him, but for all of us. I just wish I could make sense, that any of us could make sense of this. Of what has happened, of what might still happen.*

That is when he heard it. No, he did not hear a voice actually; he sensed a presence. It was a calming and reassuring presence. It seemed to say, "Fear not. All will be well. All will be revealed." James thought he had heard that voice or sensed the same feeling of relief and being removed from danger once before, but he was having trouble remembering when or where. Then it occurred to him: the apostles had been with Jesus in a boat crossing the Sea of Galilee. A storm had blown up unexpectedly and was tossing the boat about severely. Even the seasoned hands like James and John were frightened. He recalled how one of them had woken an exhausted Jesus and screamed about how they were all in peril. Jesus had just looked at all of them and shown the same sense, the same "fear not, all will be well" perspective as he stood and spoke to the winds and the waves; and immediately, there was nothing more than a mild breeze and calm seas.

How James longed to see his Master again, to hear reassuring words to fear not for all would be well. Yet as he sat there, James still felt something akin to the words and action of Jesus stirring his heart now, calming the storm within him and giving him hope a safe harbor, indeed, lay ahead.

FIFTEEN

THE THIRD DAY

The earthquake was not particularly severe, but it was enough to jolt Mary awake from what had been a sound sleep in her room at Joseph's house. She awoke facing the wall and groggily turned over so she could look out of the window at the top of the opposite wall. She decided that, based on the emerging light, it was around dawn. Then she noticed out of the corner of her eye there was another source of light in the room; it was coming from the direction of the foot of her cot. She sat up, suddenly very awake as she tried to connect what her eyes saw and what her brain was telling her. "That's not possible."

For at the foot of her bed stood her son, Jesus, smiling with his arms outstretched. Then she heard his voice. "Mother!" Still not certain what was happening, she jumped up from the bed and into his arms. The embrace they shared helped her determine that she was holding and being held by a real person, but how could it be him? Then she heard him speak again. "Do not be afraid, Mother, it is truly me." At the same time, she pushed back slightly from Jesus as she recalled all he had been through a few days before.

I don't want to hurt him and maybe reopen some of his wounds, she thought to herself.

"What's wrong, Mother?" Jesus asked, knowing full-well what was on Mary's mind.

"I-I don't want to hurt you, son. The wounds on your back and…" She looked up to see Jesus smiling, seemingly on the verge of a laugh.

"My wounds are no more, Mother, with the exception of these," he said as he showed her his hands and his feet. The places on his body where the nails had been driven now glowed like rubies. "And here." He touched his hand to his side where the lance had pierced him. "They cause me no pain. The world and all who are in it can hurt me no more, Mother."

Mary was trying to absorb all that was being said, but at the same time, she was also trying to absorb the realization her son was not dead. She recognized her son—that was true—but the physical presence in front of her bore little resemblance to the shattered body she'd just seen two days ago hanging from a cross and then holding that shattered body in her arms for what then seemed to be one last time. Now it was clear that the only scars from his torture and mistreatment of a few days ago were the ones he pointed out to her. She looked at them and then gently touched his hair and his scalp. They too glowed with a vitality she had never before seen.

His skin was totally unblemished; there was no trace of the torn flesh caused by the long thorns. At this point, all she could think of was for the two of them to be more comfortable. She hugged him once again and then took both of his hands in hers. "Come, Jesus, sit by me here on the bed like we used to do so many years ago," she said as she pointed to the bed behind her. Jesus smiled, allowed his mother to guide him to the bed, made sure she was comfortable, and then sat down beside her.

She noticed how peaceful yet confident he looked. She had seen that look a few times before in his life, although, she had to admit, not in the past few months. Then it had been constantly a look of seriousness, even tension, and what she could only describe as a sense of resignation to some impending event. He smiled as she became aware of him recognizing what she was thinking.

"You knew this was going to happen," she said. Jesus nodded. "You knew all that you were going to go through, all that you were going to suffer, and yet you said nothing, did nothing." Again, Jesus smiled.

"Yes, Mother, I knew. It was not easy, and I have to tell you that at one point I asked my Father to let me avoid it, to not let it happen. The worst part was the loneliness—being abandoned by my disciples after our Passover seder, being alone in the Roman cell. I even wondered if my Heavenly Father had abandoned me, if even he had deserted me. But then I remembered I was here to do his will, not mine. I also knew what was beyond the events of Friday, to include seeing you again." He gently squeezed her hands and kissed her forehead, bringing at last a smile to her as well. "That foreknowledge helped make it much easier to bear."

"But how, how can you be here, son? Are you a dream? Am I dreaming? I mean"—tears started to fill her eyes—"I saw you killed. I watched you die." Jesus again patted her hands and then pulled up the white robe he was wearing and again showed her the nail marks in his arms.

"What you saw was real, Mother, just like I am real, and alive, with you here now." She again noticed how the wounds, while healed, glowed like jewels. She reached out hesitantly to touch them the way a mother would touch her child's injury, wanting to comfort the child, to help make the hurt go away. "You can touch them. As I said earlier, nothing and no one can hurt me, or you, any more. Go ahead, please." Prodded by him, Mary gently touched his right hand and then, as she looked at it and smiled at her son, just as she gently raised his hand to her lips and kissed it. Her actions were once again rewarded by his radiant smile.

"I see and I believe, Jesus, but I am having trouble understanding how this is happening."

"I know this is somewhat overwhelming for you, Mother, but I also know you accept much on faith just as you did so many years ago when the angel came to you and asked you to be my mother. Just as you knew something special would happen at the wedding in Cana when you came to me—not the stewards, but to me, a carpenter's son, and *your* son—to tell me the wedding party had run out of wine. You somehow knew I could help, and you were right, weren't you?" Mary smiled and nodded in agreement.

"It is interesting that you chose that particular event, son. I was actually thinking about it the other day. And yes, you are right. I accepted on faith then you could help, and I accept on faith now you are here. I don't really understand how, but I rejoice that you are!"

Jesus smiled and took her hands. "My death and my resurrection today. Both of these events are why I came from our Heavenly Father, Mother. The death was the end of the old way of worshipping him. My resurrection is the beginning of the new way. All who follow this new way, they too some day will be raised from the dead. But to be raised from the dead, one has to first die to the old ways and to life itself.

"My death was a symbol of both of those. My resurrection will be the foundation of hope upon which all who follow my teachings can build a new life, a better, happier and faith-based life which ultimately leads them to my Father, and to their reward. Not in this life, not rewards as we have known them here. Not earthly treasure, but treasure they will store up in heaven to be enjoyed by them with my Father and me, and you."

Mary looked at him quizzically. "Me?"

"Most certainly you, Mother. You have already been shown the way ahead. You have lived a preview of what all who chose to follow me will find. You will be a model, a guide for them as they will be able to look at you, study your life and the way you always said yes to whatever my Father asked of you, and the reward you gained as a result of your faith and your obedience to his will.

"Remember what you said when the angel asked you to be my mother? 'Behold the handmaid of the Lord; be it unto me according to thy word.'[11] As you said when you visited my aunt Elizabeth after the angel visited you, 'henceforth all generations shall call me blessed. For he that is mighty hath done to me great things; and holy is his name.'"[12]

Mary looked at Jesus and smiled. "How do you know these things, Jesus? Why, you had not even been born yet, but it as if you were then when they happened."

"I am and always have been one with my Father, Mother. That is how I was able to endure the pain of last week, in particular, as I have always been with him, and he has always been with me." He took her hands. "I know this is difficult to understand now, but I promise you, soon you and my apostles will receive a gift from my Father which will help you understand all of this and much more."

Mary's eyes widened, and then she blinked a couple of times as she thought about her son's apostles. "Do you know where they are, son?"

"I do, Mother. I am going to them soon, but I had to see you first. You are the first person to see me as a resurrected man. It is one of the rewards from my Father for your faith. Many more rewards will follow, I promise you."

Mary pursed her lips slightly. "Son, I know they will all be both frightened and glad to see you. But one who needs to see you is Mary Magdalene. She was here visiting yesterday, and she did not seem to be able to get beyond your death." Mary looked at her hands in her lap and then at Jesus. "As sad as I was the last couple of days, I still felt something else was going to happen. I didn't know what, and I surely did not expect this. This is so much more than I could have hoped for." She took Jesus's hands again. "But Mary, she does not seem to have, I don't know, the ability to hope for something better."

"I know, Mother, and know this. I will see her on my way to the room where the apostles are gathered. My Father has great things in store for her as well. Her current doubt will be turned into a pillar of faith, and she will be honored from this time forward."

Mary smiled again. "I'm glad. I very much like her, son. I really do."

"Be at peace, Mother. Friday was not the end, but the beginning. All is well. You will be a witness, my witness to the beginning of a new way of living, a new faith that will be, as you were told so many years ago before I was born, the beginning of my Father's reign here on earth. You will see the building of a new city, a new Jerusalem. But it will not be a city built of stone and wood and mortar, it will be a city built of men and women over the coming centuries who have and will listen to and follow my words as taught to them by those, like my apostles and Mary Magdalene and many others, who chose to follow me."

Jesus smiled again at his mother. *He is so happy and confident*, she thought to herself. Jesus smiled at her thoughts.

"You will see me many times over the next few weeks before I finally return to my Father in heaven, Mother."

The thought of losing Jesus again was quickly salved when he added, "And I will be with you in your most magnificent heart forever. We may not be physically together at some point in the near future, Mother, but we will never be parted again." Another statement that she found hard to understand but easy to accept.

If Jesus said we were going to be apart and together, then we will be apart and together, she thought to herself. *After all, here he is sitting beside me, back from the dead. How hard can it be for him to be with me and apart from me after that?* Jesus laughed as he read her thoughts, and Mary, realizing what had just happened, laughed as well. It was the first time she had laughed in many weeks, and it felt wonderful. Jesus stood. "I will be back soon, Mother. We have much more to talk about."

Mary stood and hugged her son. "I cannot tell you how happy I am, Jesus. How very happy I am to be able to hold you, my son, again." Jesus hugged her back and then kissed her on the forehead.

"I am happy too, Mother. For once again, I have both a Father and my mother." With that, he was gone from her sight, but she felt him near, nevertheless, as she sat back down on her cot and tried to take in all that had just happened. As she sat there, she suddenly realized she was hungry. Something caught her peripheral vision, and as she looked to her right, there was a table set with bread, fruit, and a pitcher of water, just as it had been yesterday morning when she awoke.

SIXTEEN

Mary Magdalene had risen at first light, determined to somehow get into Jesus's tomb to ensure his body was properly washed and anointed. She could not recall all of the burial preparations that Joseph had hastily conducted after Jesus's death. She had been too overcome with grief to really observe and absorb what had gone on other than seeing his body placed in the tomb, the stone rolled in front of it, and, later, the appearance of the guards. As she walked toward the tomb, she easily balanced a jug of water on her head while she held cloths and oils in a sack thrown over her left shoulder. Her veil was pulled so far forward it all but hid her face from any passerby's sight.

During her walk, two thoughts kept repeating over and over in her mind—how she was going to get past the guards, and how she could get the stone moved from the entrance of the tomb. Suddenly, she realized that one issue might answer the other. *Perhaps one or more of the guards will recognize me and move the stone in return for "past favors,"* she thought to herself. That buoyed her spirits, but she still decided to be cautious and first observe the front of the tomb from the point on the hill where Joseph had spotted her yesterday.

From there, she knew she could see the tomb without being spotted herself.

She reached the viewing point, looked at the tomb, and was immediately seized with feelings of horror and grief; the stone had been rolled away from the entrance. In fact, the stone appeared to have cracked into several large pieces, providing easy and direct entrance into the tomb. And there were no guards anywhere. Forgetting her original purpose, she dropped the sack and the jug—which shattered, splashing water and dirt on to her garment—as she ran to the tomb. She did not enter it but looked inside. Jesus's body was gone. The shock was too much for her, and she fell to her knees.

Her mind was reeling. Had the guards cracked open the tomb and stolen his body? Had there been some sort of a raid by Jesus's followers, and they had driven off the guards and taken the body? She looked around the ground in front of the tomb. She saw nothing to indicate any sort of a struggle. In fact, it looked as if the guards had left in haste as some of their cloaks were scattered about the ground.

Suddenly, she sensed someone was standing behind her. Startled, she turned and fell back. All she could see was a silhouette as whoever it was had the early morning sun to their back. Thoroughly confused, she thought maybe this was some sort of a caretaker. Based on how the individual towered over her, she guessed it was a man. It never occurred to her it could be someone who could do her harm. She regained some level of composure, at least enough to stammer out a request. "Please, sir. Do you know what happened here? Do you know who took the body of the man who was inside this tomb?" She still could not make out the person's face. He had not moved but was now facing her, owing to the way she was half-sitting and half-kneeling on the ground.

"Why do you ask, woman?" a man's voice asked her.

She paused before she answered as the voice sounded familiar, but she could not recall of whose voice it reminded her. "Because he was my friend. I saw him buried here." She pointed to the rock. "I saw that stone rolled in front of the entrance after his body was in there. I wanted to come and anoint his body today. But the guards"—her arm made a sweeping gesture—"the guards who were here are gone. His body is gone. Do you know where they have taken his body?"

"Mary!" was all he said.

Suddenly, she recognized who it was—Jesus. Fear, confusion, joy—all intermingled in the woman. Joy won out as she threw herself at his feet. "Rabbi!" she blurt out as she wrapped her arms and body around the bottom of his cloak. She simultaneously burst into tears as she tried to absorb what was happening. The man whom she had seen killed and buried two days earlier was now standing over her, his hand resting gently on her head. It was almost too much to bear, and yet she realized she was, in fact, able to comprehend and accept what her senses were telling her.

"Come, Mary. Stand up," he said to her as he extended his arm to help her up. It was then she noticed the wound in his arm. Like his mother, all she could think of was how the wound, which was fully healed, glowed.

It looks like a large ruby, she thought to herself as her eyes went back and forth between Jesus's hands and his smiling face. As she stood, she looked down at his cloak; it was spotless. It should have been filthy from where the mud had splashed up onto her clothes when she dropped the water jug. Then she looked at her own cloak; it was clean as well. Dumbfounded, she looked at Jesus then at her own clothes, then at Jesus again as if to ask how.

Jesus smiled. "This world no longer has any power over me, Mary. It will be so, as well, for all those who choose to follow me." He looked at her intently yet gently. "It will be so for you, Mary." Instantly, Mary felt a rush of confidence and faith she'd never before experienced.

"How can I serve you now, Master?" she heard herself ask, still trying to comprehend all that was occurring despite her newfound faith and courage.

"Go to my apostles in the city, Mary. Tell them you have seen me, the resurrected me, and ask Peter and John to come back here with you." Mary shook her head yes and turned to leave. She then turned back to Jesus, grabbed his right hand, and kissed it.

"Forgive my lack of faith in you earlier, Jesus." Jesus smiled.

"What I ask of my followers is not easy, Mary. It will be a difficult road for most of them. But the reward which my Heavenly Father has in store for them at the end of their journey will make the hardest times worth the effort. I assure you of that, Mary. You will have your own path to follow, and it will be one which will have your name and your memory linked forever to a show of faith and charity unlike any that was seen during my time here."

Mary smiled, stifled an impulse to wave good-bye to Jesus, turned, and started to walk then run toward the city. She had not asked him where the apostles were; she knew she would be shown the way.

SEVENTEEN

Most of the apostles were still in the room where they had eaten their last meal with Jesus. John was gone, presumably to Joseph's house. Thomas had just left to buy some fresh vegetables, meat, and wine for the group. Those who remained looked at each other in a way none of them could articulate. It was as if each of them felt something special was going to happen to them this day, but none of them knew what that might be. They didn't have to say anything to each other about their feelings. They had been together long enough to sense when they had a common thought amongst themselves; all knew this was one of those times.

The soft knock on the door a couple of hours after daybreak startled them as they knew Thomas would bang on the door as if to knock it down when he returned. This sounded more like the knock of a child or a woman. When Nathaniel partially opened the door, he had the answer; there stood Mary Magdalene. The glow she exuded and the look on her face made him automatically think she was somehow tied to what they all were anticipating. He opened the door fully, and Mary practically flew into the room, her eyes searching for Peter, who was standing not far from the table where he had spent most of the last two days. She ran toward him.

"Peter! I have seen the Lord! He is alive. I saw him, Peter. I saw Jesus!"

Peter was somewhat taken aback, and all he could ask was, "Seen who, Mary?"

"Jesus! I have seen our Master, Jesus, Peter! He is alive! I saw him by the tomb." Now all the other apostles moved closer to hear what she was saying; she had their undivided attention. "I went there early this morning, hoping to be able to wash and properly anoint his body. I hadn't figured out how I would get the stone moved, but when I got there, the stone was already moved. In fact, it's broken into several very large pieces.

"I looked in the tomb, and it was empty. As I was sitting there, crying, a man came up behind me and startled me. I thought it was a caretaker or a gardener, but when I asked him if he knew where Jesus's body was, all he said to me was 'Mary,' and I knew it was the Master."

"But...but..." Peter stammered. "How can that be? Are you sure it was him?"

"Yes! He showed me his hands and his wounds. They glow like jewels, Peter, like brilliant jewels! Then he spoke to me of what his Heavenly Father, as he referred to him, has planned for all who follow him. And he asked me to come and tell you I had seen him, and for you and John to come back to the tomb with me."

Peter stood there, a sea of emotions raging inside him: hope this might be true, fear of confronting Jesus and having to explain his own betrayal of him, and joy that his friend may, indeed, be alive again. He looked around for John, and as if on cue, the other apostle walked through the door.

John immediately sensed something important had happened, and he was quickly informed of what Mary had just told the group. He looked at Mary, thinking to himself, *This cannot be the same woman who visited with Jesus's mother yesterday. She is so full of life and joy now!*

Mary was speaking. "Something else to help you know it is really Jesus, Peter. I had brought a jug of water with me to wash his body. When I saw the open tomb, I dropped the water and mud splashed all over my clothes. When I recognized Jesus, I hugged the hem of his garment. When he told me to stand up, there was no dirt, no mud, no stains whatsoever on his cloak." She looked down unconsciously at her own garments. "Nor, as you can see, on mine."

Peter was convinced. "John, Jesus has asked you and me to accompany Mary back to the tomb." John nodded his agreement.

"What about the guards, Mary? Are they still there?" asked one of the other apostles. Mary shook her head.

"No, they were all gone when I got there. Some of them left their cloaks there. It looks like they left in a hurry."

"And they may return the same way, Peter," said one of the group. Peter shook his head no.

"If Jesus has truly risen from the dead, I am sure they were all scared out of their wits and ran back to the temple." He thought for a moment. "I doubt anyone from the Sanhedrin will come out to inspect the tomb.

They will just make up their own story about what happened. No, it is time to face whatever our Master is asking of us."

Then the other nine started to object; they wanted to see Jesus too. Peter held up his hands. "My friends, we all know Jesus was always very specific in his guidance to us. If he wants just John and me, it is for a reason. Let us not start disobeying him now!" The others reluctantly shook their heads in agreement and cleared a path to the door for Peter, Mary, and John.

Peter turned as he reached the door. "Peace to all of you. We will be back soon." He was the last one to walk through the door, and then he closed it behind him.

EIGHTEEN

John, being younger (and slimmer) than Peter, arrived at the tomb first. He looked into the tomb but did not enter it, waiting for the older man who was not far behind him. When Peter arrived, he walked into the tomb with no hesitation. John followed him in. Both saw the slab where he assumed Jesus's body had been placed; it was clean, no blood or stains of any kind on it. Peter looked to one side and saw the burial clothes rolled up. He walked over to them, picked one of them up, and carefully unrolled it. It too was clean; in fact, it was almost dazzling in its cleanliness. He gently refolded the cloth and placed it back on the ground with the others. He looked at John with a quizzical expression, trying to hide what he thought must seem like a grin as both men tried to absorb what they were seeing.

Neither said anything as they came out of the tomb, looking at Mary who had stayed outside. She was looking around as if she were trying to find something or someone. "What is it, Mary? What are you looking for?" Peter said.

"Not what, Peter, who. I am looking for Jesus." She looked at and pointed to the ground just a few feet in front of the tomb. "Here. It was right here that I spoke with him, Peter. Right at this spot." All three looked at the ground. It was dry—no mud, no puddles from the spilled water of which Mary had spoken. Peter and John also started to look around when Peter suddenly saw a man coming toward them. Like Mary earlier in the morning, he could not make out the man's face as he was walking toward them with the morning sun right behind him. Peter noticed, however, this man almost seemed to glow himself. As he drew within earshot of the trio, the man spoke. "Why are you here? What are you looking for, my friends?" Peter looked quickly at the other two who stood together, a few feet away from him. Mary showed no sign of recognition of the stranger.

"We seek the man who was buried in there, sir." Peter half turned and pointed to the now-empty tomb.

As the man continued to walk toward them, he spoke again. "Why do you seek the living among the dead, Peter?"

That voice! It is the Master! Peter thought to himself, and immediately, he fell to his knees. John and Mary recognized Jesus at the same time, but both were unsure of how to react. Jesus walked directly up to Peter and, while not ignoring them, was clearly interested in talking only to the other apostle at this moment. So they stood silently and tried to listen, but they could not hear what followed. Yet neither of them was concerned he and she could not hear.

Jesus stood in front of the kneeling Peter, who had all but prostrated himself on the ground. This was a moment he had both longed for and dreaded. "Peter," he heard Jesus call to him, and he looked up. The face he looked at was smiling and relaxed. This was not a face of retribution or hate or reproach; it was the face of joy and peace.

"Yes, Lord?"

"Peter, do you love me?"

"Yes, Lord, I do."

"Feed my lambs, Peter." And he extended his hand to help the kneeling man up. Peter stood, trembling slightly but once again face-to-face with his friend, his Master. Jesus reached out his hand and put it on Peter's shoulder.

"Peter, do you love me?"

"Yes, Lord, I do." Out of the corner of his eye, Peter caught a glimpse of the wound in Jesus's right hand. He shuddered involuntarily, not out of revulsion at the sight of the wound, for he too thought it glowed like a jewel. Rather, he shuddered at the thought that somehow he had been part of the cause of the wound. Jesus felt Peter's shudder and tightened his grip ever-so-slightly on the other man's shoulder in a show of compassion and support.

"Tend my sheep."

Peter felt a weight being lifted from his heart as he heard Jesus's words. He was still trying to comprehend what was happening. It was almost like a dream. *Almost*, he thought to himself, *like when Jesus took us to the mountaintop and changed before our eyes.* His own eyes widened. *Yes, that is it!* he thought to himself. *That is where I have seen Jesus like this before. He looked like this as he spoke to Moses and Elijah. They were alive, and he was alive and glorified as he is here today!*

113

Peter shook his head and looked again at the face of the man whom he loved and trusted. He looked into the face of the man whom he had betrayed and saw nothing but love and compassion in that face.

Jesus now had both of his hands on Peter's shoulders. "Peter, do you love me, do you love me more than any of these others?"

Peter's temper and impatience began to flare slightly. *He knows how I feel,* he thought to himself. *Why does he keep asking me the same question? Why does he ask me something he knows, asking me three times.* Peter looked up in shock and embarrassment. He suddenly understood why he was being asked this question three times. It was his opportunity to make up for his three denials. The feeling of forgiveness, relief, and joy that seized him caused him to grasp both of Jesus's arms and reply in a most heartfelt manner. "Lord, you know I love you." Jesus smiled and squeezed the arms of the big man in return.

"Feed my sheep." It was all over; all had been forgiven with three simple questions. The self-recrimination, the fear, the sense of having betrayed someone whom he loved—the guilt was gone. It was all gone in an instant. Peter wept again; this time with tears of joy as he was hugged by his friend and master. Jesus put his arm around Peter and gently guided him toward Mary and John. He patted Peter's shoulder, releasing his grip on the man and moved to hug John. John was overcome with joy and was actually being held up by Jesus as his legs gave out with the shock and emotion he was experiencing.

"Thank you for taking care of our mother, John. I have seen her, and all is well with her." Jesus whispered into John's ear. "Your experiences, your voice will resonate through the years, John, and be part of the foundation of my new covenant here on Earth." Jesus pulled back slightly from John so both men could see the other's face.

The light, the glow from him. It is so beautiful, so warm, and so consoling, John thought to himself. *He is truly a light in this world, a light unto this world*

Mary was smiling, almost grinning out of joy in seeing Jesus again and realizing some measure of relief what she had experienced earlier this morning was real. Here he was, standing and talking with two of his other friends as well as her. *No*, she thought to herself. *What I experienced earlier was real. This is real. Jesus is alive! He is raised from the dead!* Involuntarily, she looked to her left, at the tomb. *I saw him buried*, she thought to herself. Then she looked back to her right at Jesus, who was just a few feet from her, smiling and even laughing with Peter and John. *And now he is here, alive…alive.* It was almost beyond comprehension.

Jesus sensed her thoughts, looked at her, and smiled. *He always had the most reassuring smile*, Mary thought to herself. *Now, it is as if that smile can solve any problem. It's just a smile, but one which seems powerful yet so peaceful and so calming all at the same time.*

"Mary, what you are seeing is not my smile, but the love, peace, and care of my Father. He and I are one." He looked at all three as they tried to understand what he had just said, but clearly, it was still beyond their comprehension. Yet none of them were concerned or upset by their lack of understanding. "Soon another gift from my Father, his Holy Spirit, will visit and be bestowed on all of you, on all of the apostles." Jesus looked specifically at Mary. "And you, Mary. Then you will understand all I am now saying and all that I said before."

Turning to Peter, he said, "Peter, I want you and John to go back to the room of our last supper together and wait for me there. I will come to you soon." Both men nodded their acknowledgement of his request. Then he turned to Mary Magdalene. "Mary, please go to Joseph of Arimithea's house. Say nothing to him or his staff. It is not yet time for them to know about me. But they will allow you in, and go to my mother." Mary smiled at the thought of visiting again with Jesus's mother, this time for a very happy reason, and nodded to his request.

Jesus smiled at them again. "I will see you all again soon. Until then, the peace of my Father be with you." Suddenly, he had vanished; not walked away, just vanished. The three looked at each other, and all impulsively reached out to grasp the others' hands. Despite what they had just witnessed, none of them questioned the wonder of it. They just smiled at each other, nodded good-bye, and set off in the direction of the places to which Jesus had asked them to go. It was now about midmorning, and while there was still a chill in the air, each of them walked off warm in body, with their hearts on fire but their minds at peace. None more so than Peter, who, as John looked over at his companion, seemed like a man renewed and one ready to take on the world and win.

NINETEEN

Caiaphas thought there might be an issue when he arrived at the temple offices to find the leader of the guards assigned to watch over Jesus's tomb nervously pacing in the hallway outside the chief priest's study. "Peace be with you, Aaron." The other man turned and bowed as Caiaphas approached and walked past him while motioning him to follow to a more private location within the temple offices. He also motioned for his chief aide, Daniel, to join the other man in the inner part of his study. As he sat on a bench, he motioned both men closer.

"I understand there has been some trouble at the tomb your men were guarding, Aaron. Tell me what happened."

The guard was stunned. *How did he know about this?* he thought to himself, forgetting that Caiaphas prided himself on being well informed on anything dealing with the Jews and the Romans.

"There was an earthquake earlier today, Lord Caiaphas."

"Yes, it woke me up," the chief priest said in response.

"Yes, well, the earthquake evidently caused the stone in the front of the tomb to crack and fall away. The guards at the tomb were caught by surprise at this as well as by a strong light that seemed to come from within the cave." Caiaphas looked quizzically at Aaron.

"Light from within the tomb?" he asked as he next shot a glance to Daniel as if to say "Has this man been drinking?" Daniel, sensing his master's thoughts, merely shrugged.

"Yes, Lord Caiaphas, from within the tomb. When the guards looked inside the tomb, it was empty! The body of the man Jesus was gone. My men got scared and all ran away."

"Where are they now?"

"Here, sir, in the temple, in the guard's quarters."

"Have they said anything about this to anyone?" The tone of the question frightened the guard.

"No, my Lord Caiaphas! And I have made sure they have been kept separated from the others to make certain of that."

"Good," was the only response. The guard relaxed slightly as Caiaphas sat thinking for a moment. Then the chief priest looked at Daniel. "Summon the others so we can discuss how to deal with this with the Romans." Daniel nodded, bowed slightly, and left the room. Caiaphas got up and walked over to a chest that sat against a wall of the room. With his back to the guard, he opened the chest, bent in, picked something out of it, closed it, and turned toward the guard, a small but obviously heavy bag in his right hand.

"Aaron," he said to the guard, "take this and share it with the others who were on duty this morning. Thank them for their service to their people and remind them to say nothing to anyone about this." He placed the bag in the other man's outstretched right hand. "They are to say nothing, understood? Nothing to anyone." The implied threat in the chief priest's voice was embellished by the stern look on his face, a look which struck fear into the heart of the guard.

"I understand, Lord Caiaphas, and they will too."

"Make sure they do, Aaron. Make sure of it."

"I will, sir. But how are you going to explain this to the Romans?" The piercing look of disapproval that Caiaphas gave the other man made him instantly realize he had stepped over a line that should not have been crossed. "My apologies for my insolence, Lord Caiaphas." And before the chief priest could answer, Aaron bowed and practically ran out of the room.

How indeed? Caiaphas thought to himself. *How indeed. Certainly not the silly tale this fool told, that is for sure.* Caiaphas sat down heavily on the bench that looked out toward an inner garden. He looked at the ground for a few moments as he thought about the best way to handle the situation. *No, we will tell the Romans we were concerned about the wild stories his followers had spread about him rising from the dead and that we took his body in the night and buried it in an unmarked grave outside the city*, He thought.

Yes, that's it. And we will tell them if anyone of our faith asks, the story will be it must have been his followers who stole his body as the guards slept. The Romans will like that. They love duplicity and will think we've told them the "real story" while we are telling one which casts his followers as a sect of grave robbers. Caiaphas smiled and then looked up as several members of the Sanhedrin walked into the office, summoned by Daniel to meet with the chief priest.

Caiaphas stood to greet them. Enough of them were present to satisfy his plans. "My friends, we have a minor problem to resolve. Please take your seats, and let me tell you what is going on and what I propose to do about it." He then explained to them Aaron's report, changing the time line and events to reflect a story of guards falling asleep and the body being taken at night, with the theft only being discovered fortuitously because of the earthquake breaking the stone.

The other listened and several shifted nervously as Caiaphas spoke; motions which did not go undetected by the chief priest. He knew a number of them, just like Phineas from the day before, were not comfortable with what had occurred on Friday. Well, that was their problem to resolve. Caiaphas had to protect his people from the Romans, and this was how he had decided to do it. He went on, explaining the story that was to be told to the Romans. One of the Sanhedrin, Benjamin, had the nerve to ask Caiaphas if that was what had really happened. Caiaphas was not pleased with the question but saw an opportunity to turn it to his advantage as he looked somewhat disapprovingly at the other man.

"What happened is but for a few to know, Benjamin. Be secure in the knowledge that those who know are few and safe from Roman hands. The Romans will be told what we want them to know. Nothing more."

Benjamin knew he had heard all he was going to hear about what really might have happened, so he nodded and remained quiet for the rest of the meeting. Only one other question was asked by one other in the group, and it was in regards to the guards—had they been "taken care of?" The questioner was assured by Caiaphas they had. He gave no details, just an affirmation they had been cared for.

The only thing remaining was to decide who would take this story to Pilate. The emissary would have to leave right away as the longer the time between the events of the morning and the Sanhedrin representative's meeting with Pilate, the more the chance some other rumor may spread and cause trouble. Caiaphas, of course, would not be the one to visit the governor; he had too much contempt for the Romans in general and Pilate in particular. He believed it was both beneath him and defiling for any chief priest to meet with the governor. So a representative, Joshua, one of Caiaphas's closest allies and an eloquent speaker to boot, volunteered to carry the message. He remained behind as the others were dismissed and gave their greetings to the chief priest.

Caiaphas then sat with Joshua and went over the story one more time to ensure both men were satisfied with it. Joshua then left the temple with Daniel, who would serve as translator, while Caiaphas sat and waited.

TWENTY

Normally, Pilate liked to ensure everyone who came to see him, scheduled or unscheduled, had to wait at least a half hour or so to ensure the visitor knew who was in charge. However, he had a grudging respect and admiration for the high priest if, for no other reason, the man had politely refused all invitations to meet with him. Pilate knew Caiaphas was a powerful leader, well respected by his people, unlike the puppet king Herod. So he was careful not to further alienate the man whom he saw as a "worthy adversary." It also helped that he had a great deal of admiration for Joshua, who inevitably was the chief emissary Caiaphas sent to Pilate. Joshua was a tall, handsome, and self-assured man but one who had the good sense to "play the role" of subordinate to Pilate. It also was to his favor he had a fairly good command of Latin as opposed to Pilate's meager Aramaic vocabulary. Nevertheless, it had become customary for both men to have their translators present for any meeting.

Pilate always took notice when Joshua arrived for an unscheduled meeting, so he quickly finished the papers he was reviewing and walked to the great hall of the praetorium to meet Joshua soon after he arrived. He smiled and greeted the other man warmly, although his smile was generated more by has foreknowledge of the ritual they would now go through. One man would speak, his translator would repeat the first speaker's statement, and the recipient would look to his own translator to see if what he was being told had been translated accurately. Pilate's translator, Lucius, was the master of subtlety, using only his eyebrows to signal a correct or flawed translation. If the latter, Pilate would either ask the translator to repeat his statement; or if he felt there was a real error, he would summon Lucius to whisper his version of what had just been said. Then he would mentally compare the two, trying to determine if a message was being sent or not sent by the other party.

Pilate sat on his bench and listened as Daniel, acting as Joshua's translator, respectfully asked Pilate to recall the criminal Jesus, who had been crucified a few days earlier. Lucius indicated a proper translation of what Joshua had said, and Pilate nodded his recollection. Daniel then went on to state how Caiaphas, who sent his warmest and most profound greetings to the governor, was concerned by rumors swirling after Jesus's death that his followers might try and steal his body and then claim he had risen from the dead as he had indicated he would do. Again, Lucius concurred with the translation; again, Pilate nodded understanding.

Daniel then went on to say Caiaphas was concerned about the effect such an event might have on the good order provided throughout Judea by the noble Romans, so he had given instructions for those guarding the tomb to open the tomb last night, remove the body, and rebury in an unmarked grave some distance outside the city.

Pilate listened, waited for confirmation, and finally spoke. "That seems to be a wise and prudent course of action, Joshua. Please convey my thanks and warmest regards to Lord Caiaphas for his forethought." Now it was Joshua's turn to listen as Daniel translated Pilate's comments into Aramaic, and Lucius's eyebrow indicated it had been translated correctly. Joshua bowed in acknowledgement of Pilate's compliment; in fact, he had understood what the governor had said and had already been preparing his next statement.

"My Lord Pilate, I will do that with pleasure and honor," he said. "I would respectfully ask on behalf of Lord Caiaphas if you would, therefore, ignore any rumors you might hear about this Jesus being raised from the dead. His followers are fanatics, and Caiaphas believes they will go to any length to disrupt the order and harmony in which we live under Roman rule." Lucius cocked his eyebrow on this statement, not because it was incorrectly translated, but because of the bald diplomatic "doublespeak" it contained. The Romans and the Judeans were hardly living together in harmony. But Lucius was a man of limited vision and had only one major talent—his fluency in Aramaic.

Pilate understood the real meaning of and the necessity for the political "niceties" being spoken by Joshua. He smiled, stood up, walked over to Joshua, and bowed slightly. He had learned early on in his assignment to Judea the Orthodox Jews were loath to touch or be touched by someone whom they considered to be an unclean infidel—for example, the Roman governor.

So he took no offense but rather compensated with this bow, which he felt conveyed respect while still projecting Roman dignity and authority. "Please thank Lord Caiaphas again, Joshua, for sharing this important information with me, and remind him of my enduring respect for him and my fondest hope that, one day, I might have the privilege of meeting him in person." Pilate always took advantage of any opportunity to remind Caiaphas's minions he had not forgotten this slight. Before the other man could respond, Pilate saluted, turned, and walked back in to his private chambers as the others bowed at his back and left the great hall.

Once in his office, Pilate sat down, mulling over what he'd been told. He had been somewhat troubled by the whole "Jesus" affair but had satisfied his conscience with the need to occasionally make an example of someone, and Jesus had proven useful to Pilate in that regard. And he had heard rumors of what Jesus had said about rising from the dead. For an agnostic like Pilate, who worshipped the Roman gods only because it was politically expedient to do so, the thought of an afterlife was incomprehensible. Here and now, that is what counted. That and doing the best he could to, hopefully, win the favor of Caesar and, with it, a better posting for his next assignment. That was all Pilate really believed in—the power of the emperor to make Pontius Pilate's life more comfortable in the "hereafter Judea."

As quietly and discreetly as ever, Septimus had appeared, tablet in hand, ready to take down and carry out orders or desires that Pilate might have. Pilate looked at the other man and shook his head with a wry smile on his face. "You heard, Septimus?"

"Yes, my lord," Septimus replied as he looked out toward the now-empty hall. "If you ask me, sir, I'd be willing to bet they, in fact, lost that man's body to his followers, and sooner or later, those same followers will start crowing about how he has been raised from the dead."

Pilate shook his head in agreement. "Perhaps, but either way, their story of what they supposedly did, taking his body and burying it outside the city, has some ring of truth, and even ingeniousness, to it." He shook his head. "Send for some wine, Septimus. Maybe we've heard the last of this Jesus, and maybe we've not. But I suspect if we do hear more, it will be a whisper, not a shout, and it won't last very long." Pilate then raised his hand. "And send for Gaius, the centurion. I want to have some of my own people out and about, listening for what is being said or not said about this Jesus rising from the dead.

"As you wish, sir." Septimus turned to summon one of the house servants, and Pilate was left alone with his thoughts.

How can one man, one single Judean cause so much bother and consternation? he wondered to himself.

Some moments later, Gaius was ushered into Pilate's chamber; he stood there and saluted the procurator in his full uniform. "Hail Pilate."

Pilate, who had been deep in thought over what he referred to as the "Jesus issue," was somewhat startled by the greeting and looked at the man quizzically. Then he recalled how he had sent for him. "Ah, yes, Centurion Gaius. Thank you for coming so swiftly."

"My honor and my duty, my lord Pilate." As he thought to himself, *And I had no choice anyway.*

"Yes, well, I have a very special task for you, Centurion. I want you to pick three or four of your most-trusted subordinates, and along with you, I want you to go out among the people here in Jerusalem and listen."

"Listen, my lord?"

"Yes, listen. I am told there are rumors in the city concerning the criminal Jesus, whose execution you supervised last week." The vision of the woman's face and her questioning look reappeared in Gaius mind, and he shifted slightly, not so much so Pilate could notice, but enough. Pilate was still talking. "The wildest things are supposedly being said. Things like he is not dead. He has risen from the dead. All sorts of crazy things." Gaius stifled a startled look and decided it was best to play along with what he was being told.

"Raised from the dead, my lord? How in the name of all the gods is that possible?"

Pilate looked at the other man and smiled. "Exactly, Gaius, it is not possible. But you know how these Judeans are. It doesn't take much to stir them up, and I recall I was dismissive of his followers when we last spoke. We cannot have anyone or any group disrupting the good order we, and those Romans who came before us, have achieved here in Judea."

127

"As you command, my lord. If we hear any of these rumors, what do you want us to do? Arrest those who are speaking them?"

Pilate shook his head. "No, do nothing. Try and remember who it is who says such things and report back here to Septimus within the next two hours. Any questions?" Now it was time for Gaius to shake his head.

"No, my lord. It will be done as you command." He raised his arm in salute. "Hail Caesar. Hail Pontius Pilate." Pilate returned his salute.

"You have my leave to go." Pilate looked at Septimus. "Septimus, the wine now if you please." Septimus bowed and walked out with the centurion, noting the quizzical and seemingly confused look on the other man's face as they left the room together.

"Anything wrong, Centurion?"

Startled back from his visions of that woman's face, Gaius jumped slightly. "What? Ah, no, sir. No, I am, well, I'm just trying to adjust to this notion of someone coming back from the dead. What an absurd idea."

"Yes, my thoughts exactly. I look forward to your report, Centurion," Septimus declared as he made a sharp left turn to retrieve the wine Pilate had requested.

For his part, Gaius returned to the soldiers' quarters, picked the men whom he knew he could trust with such a mission, and told each of them where he wanted the man to patrol. He then changed into civilian clothes as he thought he might hear more if he didn't stand out as he would in his uniform and headed out to the area he had selected for himself—the street on which the house of Joseph of Arimithea could be found.

Joshua was ushered into Caiaphas's chambers and reported on the meeting. His impression was it had gone well and that Pilate had accepted the story of how Jesus's body had been reburied in an unmarked grave. Caiaphas smiled as he listened to Joshua. It appeared the deception had worked. He thanked Joshua for his service and asked him to send in one of the scribes. Joshua bowed, exited the room, and was soon replaced by the chief scribe of the Sanhedrin. Caiaphas looked up at the man, somewhat startled as he had been lost in thought. He then remembered why he had summoned him. "Please bring me a scroll to read. Nothing dealing with the law." He mumbled to himself, "I've had enough of that for a while." Then he looked at the scribe again. "Pick something, say from the prophets. Pick anything, Zachary." The other man bowed, left the room, and headed for where all the scrolls were kept.

Caiaphas was again quickly lost in his thoughts. *Raised from the dead. Impossible and unbelievable. And why him of all men? Why should he think he would deserve such a blessing? No, it's beyond comprehension.* Caiaphas looked up as the scribe returned with a scroll and placed it in the high priest's lap. "Thank you, Zachary." The other man bowed, turned, and left the high priest alone in the room.

As he started to unroll the scroll, however, he couldn't shake one thought from his mind. *It's impossible, but yet…no. I can't believe I am thinking this. But what if…*

129

what if it were true? He shook his head as if that would forcibly remove the idea from his brain and looked down at the passage before him—Isaiah 53.

> But he was wounded for our transgressions, he was bruised for our iniquities: the chastisement of our peace was upon him; and with his stripes we are healed.
>
> All we like sheep have gone astray; we have turned every one to his own way; and the LORD hath laid on him the iniquity of us all.
>
> He was oppressed, and he was afflicted, yet he opened not his mouth: he is brought as a lamb to the slaughter, and as a sheep before her shearers is dumb, so he openeth not his mouth.
>
> He was taken from prison and from judgment: and who shall declare his generation? for he was cut off out of the land of the living: for the transgression of my people was he stricken.
>
> And he made his grave with the wicked, and with the rich in his death; because he had done no violence, neither was any deceit in his mouth.
>
> Yet it pleased the LORD to bruise him; he hath put him to grief: when thou shalt make his soul an offering for sin, he shall see his seed, he shall prolong his days, and the pleasure of the LORD shall prosper in his hand.
>
> Isaiah 53:5–10 (KJV)

Caiaphas stopped reading, put down the scroll, and rubbed his eyes. He looked out the window, trying to collect his thoughts. *It is not possible. It cannot be.* Despite his best efforts to the contrary, however, a stronger thought kept crowding out the others. *But… but…what if…just what if…*

TWENTY ONE

John had to practically run to keep up with Peter, who strode quickly and confidently through the city on his way to the meeting room. John was amazed Peter didn't crash into people on the narrow streets, but it appeared they saw him coming and moved out of the way versus getting run over. *I wonder what Jesus said to him to cause this change,* John thought to himself. *This is not the man whom I left last night!*

In a much shorter time than it had taken them to go to the tomb, both men stood in front of the door as Peter knocked forcefully while simultaneously announcing for all to hear that he and John were at the door. The door swung open, and Peter rushed through like a strong incoming tide. As soon as he reached the middle of the room, he became the center of attention; the others noticed the change in him as well. "Mary Magdalene was right, my friends! We two, John and I, we have seen and spoken to Jesus. He lives. He lives!" The others looked at each other somewhat incredulously and then at John who was nodding his head in affirmation of what Peter had just said. Then they all burst forth with questions.

"What does he look like?"

"What did he say?"

"Is he coming here?"

Peter held up his hands to quiet the excited group of men. "He looks the same, but he also looks different. There is a glow, a shining, about him and an air of peace yet strength." Peter looked down and then spoke again. "The wounds are there, but they are not like any wounds I have ever seen before. They shine…like jewels." More questions were shouted toward the apostle

"What did he say, Peter?"

"What did he say to you? You too look different. You look like the Peter we knew before the last several days."

Peter hesitated and then decided he had nothing more to hide. "My friends, you may recall a few days ago I said we had all betrayed him. I cannot speak for the group, but I can tell you that I-I betrayed him."

The shouts of disbelief were coming in fast. "No!"

"Not you, Peter. You were…you are his best friend."

"You could never have betrayed him, Peter. Never!"

"I could and I did, not once, but three times." The others looked at him, stunned. "Jesus was in the temple being questioned by the Sanhedrin. I sat outside by the fire and three different times—three times—others around the fire accused me of being one of Jesus's followers or of knowing him. And three times I denied I knew him. So yes, I did betray him." The room fell silent.

"But, my friends, when we saw Jesus at the grave, three times he asked he if I loved him—three times." He held up three fingers to help drive the point home. "I answered yes each time, and the last time, I was starting to get angry." He looked around at the group, which was spellbound. "I thought to myself, 'Why does he keep asking me this? He knows I love him!"

"And then it occurred to me, he was giving me the chance to repent for my denials. He was forgiving me for abandoning him." Peter looked at the floor and shook his head. "I swear to you, my friends, I will never betray him again. Never." The firmness of his voice and the fire in his eyes when he looked up at them left no doubt as to Peter's sincerity and conviction. Again, silence fell on the room until Peter's brother, Andrew, spoke up.

"Well, I, for one, am glad Jesus forgave you, Peter. Having you moping around here for the last couple of days has been damn depressing!" All of them burst into laughter as Peter grabbed Andrew and hugged his brother. Suddenly, however, their attention was drawn to the table where they had their last meal with Jesus. Their eyes were drawn to the light emanating from in front of the table, the light which shown off, or seemingly was coming from within, the white garments of Jesus as he stood by the table.

"Peace be with you!" he said as he smiled broadly and stretched out his arms toward them. Astonished and initially frightened by this sudden apparition, the others quickly followed Peter's lead when, after a moment's hesitation, they all rushed toward Jesus. As they gathered around their friend and master, it seemed as if he was able to hug each of them individually and all of them together at the same time. He made sure to embrace each one of them, whispering something meant only for that one person in each apostle's ear.

Some were transfixed by his wounds, which he willingly showed to those who were in need of "reinforcement" of their other senses. He made sure those whom he sensed wanted to touch his wounds could do so, ensuring them it would cause him no pain or discomfort. No one took him up on that offer though. His word was good enough for them. As the realization of what they were seeing and experiencing sunk in, the joy of all grew in an unbounded manner. The apostles were thrilled with the return of their Master; and the Master was thrilled and happy to again be physically among those who he loved so well.

Jesus held up his hands, and the bedlam died down. He smiled again at them as they all stood watching him, waiting to hear his voice. "We have much to talk about, my friends, my brothers. I have much to tell you. But first, let us eat." He motioned toward the table, which was set with wine, meats, fruit, and fresh vegetables sitting in jugs or on platters. Andrew looked around for Thomas, who had gone out to procure some food for them, but he'd not yet returned. The others noticed his absence as well and turned to look at each other, trying to figure out where all the food and drinks had come from. There was an unspoken sense among them. They suspected where it had emanated from, but they were still trying to absorb seeing and touching Jesus again. So the knowledge that their Lord and Master had provided this feast just didn't sink in yet.

Whatever their hesitation, it was quickly and completely dissipated as they followed Jesus to the table, sat down, and watched him pour the wine, take some meat, and eat and drink. Jesus saw he was the only one eating, so he put down the cup, looked around at them, and, smiling, said, "My friends, are you hungry or not?" That was all the encouragement they needed, and soon, they were all digging in, pouring and sharing wine. The conversations started slowly, but soon, their joy and enthusiasm started to kick in, and a rising tide of conversation interspersed with ever-more-joyful laughter filled the room.

The fishermen among the group were the first to inspire the laughter as, typical of fishermen, they started reminiscing about the best days they'd had over the years, the greatest catches, etc. As the sizes of their catches grew in their stories, Jesus would lean forward so he could look at the speaker, rest his chin on his hand, and raise his right eyebrow. That was all that was needed to bring the storyteller back down to a more-realistic level, and the howls of laughter to increase as each storyteller was gently and silently confronted by their friend and master.

The meal stretched into the early afternoon. Once the adrenalin and emotional impact of knowing Jesus was alive again had died down, Jesus slowly took over the conversation, using the time to instruct his apostles. He knew they would not immediately grasp all he was telling them, but he was "planting seeds," which would blossom fully when he and his Father would send the Holy Spirit to awaken and inspire them in a few weeks.

For now, it was time to "plow" and nourish the fertile ground of their minds and plant the seeds as well as some number of ideas that they did grasp.

After several hours, Jesus stood up and told them he must leave them for a short time. There was some initial concern among the apostles about his leaving again, but as soon as he promised them he would return before the end of the day, all fear and doubt left them. Peter looked around at the group then at Jesus. "Master, it is good for us to be here," he said.

Jesus smiled warmly at them. "Peace be with you," he replied, and then he vanished from their sight.

Despite the magnitude of the event, none of them was surprised. It was only the knocking on the door that brought their attention back to the room. One of them ran to open the door, some of them, no doubt thinking it might be Jesus. They were so emotionally drained they had no concept of how long he had been gone. It turned out to be Thomas, who immediately sensed something had happened, followed by his noticing they had clearly been eating. What they had been eating, he couldn't figure out as he was carrying several sacks of food for the group. Having been confident enough that they were in no danger from the Romans and not wanting to impose too much on Joseph of Arimithea, Thomas had left the room several hours earlier to get food for the group; these were the sacks he now placed in the floor. The confusion on his face was apparent.

"Thomas, we have seen the Lord!" one of the apostles shouted at their clearly bewildered friend.

"Where?" he asked.

"Here! Right here! He was standing here with us. He ate with us. He left not very long ago."

Thomas looked toward the door and then back at his companions. "No one passed me on my way here."

"No, you don't understand, Thomas. The door was locked and bolted yet he was suddenly among us. He talked to and touched each of us. Then he asked us to eat with him. We had a meal which came from, well, I'm not really sure where it came from, but we ate and drank and talked with him."

"Eat? How could you eat? What could you eat? There was hardly any food here! That is why I went out this morning to buy some more, remember?" Peter walked over to Thomas and put his hand on his shoulder. Thomas noticed right away Peter's mood had changed entirely; he no longer looked like a man in pain.

"Thomas, my brother. Jesus was here with us. I am sorry you missed seeing him, but I assure you he was here." He then looked at the others as he continued. "And we all really do know where the food and drink he shared with us came from. Jesus provided it for us. I don't know how, but if he can be raised from the dead, how hard can it be for him, or his Father, to provide us a meal? No, it came from him." The others all shook their heads in agreement. "He promised he would be back to visit with us later today. You will see him then, Thomas."

Thomas was still confused and a bit angry. He felt he had put himself in some jeopardy to get them food, then to have Jesus appear to them while he was not there and to feed them all as well. He just did not know what to make of all of this.

"I find it hard to believe. I go out, and to avoid any peril from the temple guards, I have to take backstreets and not stay too long at any one vendor. It takes me hours to do this and stay undetected, stay undetected to try and keep all of you safe! And I come back here to stories of Jesus appearing and food from who-knows-where. Well, when he comes again, *if* he comes again, I'll believe it when I put my fingers in his wounds." He touched his own finger to his arm. "And put my hand in his side." Again, he pointed to his own side, demonstrating what he would do. Then he walked off toward the storage area to put away the food he had brought.

The others started to disperse from near the door where they had all congregated upon Thomas's return. Some started to walk toward the table to clean it up. They stopped and pointed as it had already been cleaned and fresh jugs of water and wine had been placed on the table along with a large platter of fruit. Each man except Thomas looked at the other, shook his head, and tried to absorb what had been a most exciting and mysterious yet joyful half day.

TWENTY TWO

Mary Magdalene knocked at the door of Joseph's house, which opened almost immediately as she was welcomed in by one of the servants. He seemed to know exactly why Mary was there, escorting her directly to the room in which Jesus's mother was sitting. Both women were struck by the joy and happiness clearly showing on the other's face, and each ran to the middle of the room to greet the other. They hugged for a long time, saying nothing as both were moved to tears. Each woman moved a step away from the other and brought out a small cloth from within their garments to wipe away the tears. With their arms around each other, they moved to a corner of the room where two chairs were located, one of which Mary had been seated in when Mary Magdalene entered the room. As they sat facing each other, still holding hands, Mary broke the silence.

"You have seen my son."

Mary Magdalene enthusiastically nodded her head. "Twice. Once earlier today when I went to the tomb to wash and anoint his body. Oh, you cannot imagine the horror I felt when I saw that the stone had been rolled away from the entrance of his tomb. The guards were gone, and the tomb was empty. I was so overwhelmed with grief. I was beside myself. And then suddenly, there he was, smiling and calling me by name."

Mary nodded. "He always knows just the right time to come to the aid of those in need, doesn't he?"

"Yes, I was truly in need, Mary, but no longer. I mean I still need his love and support, but I feel he has now set my feet on solid ground." She paused and looked at the older woman, who was beaming, basking in the reflected joy of the physically beautiful woman who sat next to her, a woman who had now taken on an inner beauty as well.

Mary Magdalene continued, her joy and excitement causing her to talk much faster than normal. "He told me I would have my own path to follow." She paused and looked down, blushing slightly, but then went on. "And he told me that it will be one which will have my name and memory linked forever because of a show of faith and charity unlike any other. I have tried to remember what it is I might have done to deserve such praise, such an honor. But I cannot recall what it might have been."

Mary nodded. "I know what he is talking about. He told me about it several months ago. He had saved you from a mob which wanted to stone you for adultery." Mary Magdalene turned red and tried to hide her face in her hands. Mary touched them gently and brought them down to her lap. "There is nothing to be ashamed of, Mary. He forgave you. How can anyone else do anything less?

"Some time after that, he was having dinner with some Pharisees, and you came into the house. He told me how you washed and anointed his feet and dried them with your hair." Mary stopped and looked off in to the distance and then looked at the other woman again. "It's sad, really, but yours is the only act of kindness shown to my son of which he ever spoke. He did so many things for so many people—curing their illnesses, feeding them, ministering to them—but you are the only one, other than one leper, who ever showed him an act of kindness in return.

"I remember when he came to visit me once. He told me that in some of the towns, as stories and knowledge of him spread, they were actually demanding him to 'show them a sign.' To do something to impress and, I guess, entertain them. He was so saddened and almost…almost frustrated by their lack of courtesy, their lack of faith." She looked at Mary Magdalene and patted the other woman's hands. "That is why your act of kindness was and is so important to him. And that is why, if he said so, you will always be remembered for it."

Mary Magdalene shook her head, trying to absorb what the other Mary was telling her. At first she was embarrassed, but then her thought turned toward, *If that is how he sees me, how he wants me to help him going forward, then so be it.* The other Mary seemed to be reading her thoughts.

"It looks to me, Mary, as if you are accepting what he is asking of you. You have accepted his will." Mary Magdalene nodded.

"Yes, it is difficult in one way. I don't feel worthy of such a role. But when he looks at you and asks you something or tells you he wants you to do a particular task, how can anyone say 'no, I can't.'?"

"He often talked doing his own Father's will." Mary Magdalene looked puzzled. She knew him as the son of a carpenter. What could a carpenter "will" someone to do? Mary saw the rising confusion on the other woman's face. She reached out and touched the other woman's hands again.

"Mary, there is something you need to understand. I think you are 'aware' of this, but I need to tell you so you truly understand. Jesus is the Son of God. Joseph, my husband was his foster father. I was visited by an angel before Joseph and I were married, and the angel told me I was to bear a son and that he would be called Son of the Most High and he would rule the house of Jacob forever.

"Jesus is no ordinary man, Mary. That is why he has been raised from the dead, to bring his teachings, his way to the world. I suspect he will be with us for a while as he is now, but we will be asked by him to carry on his work after he has gone."

"Where will he go?"

"Back to his Father in heaven." Mary Magdalene's face fell. "But he will send us help to carry on his work.

"You are particularly blessed, Mary, for he has told you what your role will be. I know you will make him proud and, like all of his followers, your reward will be great. Not here on earth, not in this life. But in the life like the one in which he now lives."

Mary Magdalene sat there, absorbing what she had just been told. She knew she had mixed feelings—sadness that Jesus would be leaving soon, but confidence that this very special woman sitting across from her was telling her the truth. So she took solace in the fact that somehow, even though he was physically going to be separated from them, he would still be close to them.

Mary recognized the other woman's inner conflict and once more patted her hands. "I know this is all very startling, Mary, and hard to understand. But we will get through this together, along with his apostles and all those who believe in him. And in our lifetime, we will watch as something wonderful takes root and starts to grow—his kingdom here on earth."

There was a soft knock on the door as one of Joseph's servants called and asked to be admitted. Mary acknowledged the request, and the door opened to reveal the servant nervously shifting from one foot to the other. "Yes, Isaac, what is it?" Mary asked.

"There is a man at the door, my lady, a man asking about your son, Jesus. I'm not certain, but I do not think he is a Judean even though he has tried to dress like one. He does not know that you are here. Should I just send him away or tell him to return when my master is back home?"

Mary thought for a second and recalled the words Jesus had spoken to her earlier in the day, something to the effect that no one could ever harm him or her again. "No, Isaac, let him in. I...we, Mary and I, will meet him in the garden. Please give us a few minutes to get there."

"As you wish, my lady," Isaac replied as he closed the door. The two women got up, straightened out their garments, walked away from the front of the house, where the stranger was still standing, and entered

Joseph's garden. They sat together on a small stone bench that faced the direction where the stranger would approach them.

Mary immediately recognized the man's face, and, after a split second's hesitation, smiled as she suspected he was not here in an "official" capacity. Mary Magdalene, on the other hand, was shocked and scared when she too recognized his face and grabbed Mary's hand and arm. But when she looked at Mary, her terrified gaze was met with one of peace and calm, as if to say, "Fear not." Mary's composure helped the younger woman somewhat, but not completely, as she found herself still shaking with fear but hoping it would not be noticed by the stranger.

For his part, it wasn't until he was a few feet from the women that Gaius recognized both of them from Jesus's crucifixion. He stopped, his own face filled with horror, confusion, and shame. Yet as he looked at Mary, he found the woman's question, which had tormented him, had suddenly turned from "Do you know what you have done?" to "I can help you understand what you have done, and I can help you." He bowed to the two women and, through Isaac who was serving as the interpreter, introduced himself as Centurion Publius Gaius. Mary introduced herself as the mother of Jesus and pointed to Mary Magdalene, stating that she was one of Jesus's followers. Despite being a hardened combat veteran, Gaius was more nervous standing in front of these two women than he had ever been facing any enemy. Mary sensed his fear and discomfort.

145

"How can we help you, Publius Gaius?" she said. "Please sit over there." She pointed to a bench across from the women. "And tell us why you are here."

Gaius turned around and half stumbled onto the bench. He wrung his hands in front of himself, and the more nervous he became, the calmer Mary Magdalene was as she sensed more and more this man posed no threat to them. For his part, Isaac stood mute, his mouth open, but no words came forth from his lips. That was because he was listening to Mary speaking in Aramaic as Gaius responded in Latin. Yet both individuals seemed to be hearing and responding to the other as if they were speaking in a common tongue. Finally, after what seemed like a very long time, Gaius spoke again.

"I-I do not know where to start, my lady. I think you know who I am, the man who was in charge of the Romans who crucified your son, Jesus."

"Yes, I recognized you as that person, Gaius."

"Yes, well, since that day…" He paused again, but then Mary's gaze was so comforting, so seemingly full of understanding he realized that he could and had to tell her all. "Well, since that day, I have been haun—I have kept remembering something your son said from the cross. Something about asking his father to forgive them for they know not what they do. And then I remembered the look on your face when we put his body in your arms. It was a look that, to me, said, 'Do you know what you have just done?' And I tell you in truth, my lady, I have not been able to drive either those words or the image of your face from my mind."

Mary nodded in understanding, and Gaius knew he must go on. He also realized for the first time he had been speaking to her in Latin and she had been responding in kind. That startled him for a moment. Then just assuming she was fluent in Latin, he went on. Isaac stood transfixed as he witnessed this linguistic miracle, having been reduced to the role of a spectator.

"Yesterday, I had a feeling I might find the answer to those questions here." He swept his arm in a wide arc. "Somewhere here in the streets of Jerusalem. Somehow, I wound up on the other side of the street, looking in the direction of this garden."

"I spent most of yesterday here in the garden, Gaius, It helped me as I grieved for my son." Gaius lowered his head and shook it. "But I no longer grieve." That caused Gaius to snap his head up as he tried to comprehend what Mary had just said.

"Why, why do you say that, ma'am? That you no longer grieve for your son?"

"Because, Gaius, my son lives. He has been raised from the dead."

Gaius's head was swimming. "But, but that cannot be!" he stammered.

"It is the truth, Gaius. I have seen him and spoken to him in this very house." Mary pointed to the other woman. "Mary Magdalene has seen him as well, twice this morning." The other Mary nodded her agreement. She was still too nervous to speak. Gaius was close to being in shock as he tried to absorb what he had just been told.

"But how? When?"

"This morning. He had told us before his death he would rise on the third day. At the time, to be honest, none of us really knew what that meant. Like you now, we could not understand what he was telling us. But this morning, just as he had foretold, today is the third day, and he has risen from the dead and has been appearing to those to whom he is closest."

"Then the rumors are true?" Gaius exclaimed.

"Rumors?"

"Yes, my lady. I was asked—no, commanded—by the Roman procurator Pontius Pilate to walk the streets and listen to the rumors of this man Jesus being alive again after we had killed him. I thought it was just a bunch of nonsense being spread by you Judeans." He held his hands out toward the women. "But your conviction, your…your, well, just the way you are sitting here, calmly telling me, the man who commanded the troops who killed your son, telling me he is alive. Well, it is just too fantastic to comprehend!"

Mary nodded. "Yes, it is a lot to comprehend, Gaius." She looked at him with an intense but kind gaze. "It is probably hard for you to believe because you really didn't know my son, did you?"

Gaius shook his head. "Well, let me tell you about my son and help you believe in him, in his message, and the future he has promised us all."

I think my life is about to change, he thought as Gaius leaned forward, eager to hear what this truly remarkable woman had to say to him.

TWENTY THREE

It was late in the afternoon of the third day when there was a knock on the door of the room where the apostles were still gathered. Several of the apostles jumped up and ran toward the door, thinking that it might be Jesus returning as he had promised. They were somewhat disappointed when they opened the door, and there stood two of the men who had followed Jesus loyally for over a year now, Cleopas and Isaac. It was clear from the excitement on their faces something most notable had occurred, and they could barely contain themselves as they waited for the door to be closed, and they turned to face Peter and the others. "Peter, we have seen the Lord! We have seen Jesus!"

"Where did you see him?" Peter asked.

"We were on our way to Emmaus, walking along the road when he joined us. For some reason, we did not recognize him, not at all. He walked with us for a while, and he asked us what we had been talking about when he joined us." Isaac, the speaker, pointed to the other man. "Cleopas asked him how he did not know about all that had happened to the Master, about his crucifixion and death. We figured this man must be a stranger if he'd not heard of these things.

"Then he shook his head and told us how foolish we were for not recognizing what all the prophets had spoken of before. And he proceeded to patiently interpret for us all of the prophecies concerning Jesus. Oh, Peter, our hearts were burning as this remarkable man spoke to us. He walked with us for some time until we entered the village which had been our destination. It appeared he was going to walk on, but we asked him to stay and eat with us, given the late hour of the day, and he agreed.

"As we sat at table with him and he pronounced the blessing, broke the bread, and gave it to us, our eyes were opened, and we recognized him as Jesus! Then he suddenly disappeared. We got up and came right back here to share this wonderful news with you!"

Peter nodded and smiled. "Thank you, and we share in your joy and wonder for we have seen Jesus as well."

"Where, Peter?"

"At his tomb, and earlier today, here in this room. He sat and ate with us as well. He told us he would be back later today, and we are here waiting for his return." Peter and all the others in the room turned as a sudden light behind them drew their attention to the other side of the room; there stood Jesus.

"Peace be with you." All in the room save Thomas rushed to greet Jesus. For his part, Thomas stood, mouth agape, almost unable to move. After a few minutes, as the greetings had died down, Jesus walked over to Thomas, who now started to shake with fear and anticipation as Jesus drew nearer.

"Thomas, my brother, please"—Jesus pulled up the sleeve of his garment to expose the wound in his wrist—"put your finger in my hand." At the same time, with his other hand, he moved his garment to one side to expose the lance wound in his side. "Here, place your hand in my side, so you will no longer persist in your unbelief. I am here, Thomas. It is me. I am alive, and I am real."

Thomas covered his eyes with his hands and started to sink to his knees as a combination of sincere reverence and some shame overcame him. "My Lord and my God."

Jesus reached down and helped the man to his feet, clasping him by his arms. "Be at peace, Thomas. You are blessed because you believe, now that you have seen me and talked to me after my resurrection." Jesus looked up at the others standing in the room. "But blessed are those who, in the future, will not have seen me and yet will still believe." He looked back at Thomas. "You and the others will help them believe, Thomas." Jesus looked around at his apostles. "That is the mission and the joy which I will leave with all of you.

"I will soon be going back to my Father in heaven, but I assure you, you will not be left alone to carry out this very special task. My Father will send his Spirit to enlighten and guide you. The road ahead for you all will be hard and difficult. For many of you, the journey will be at the forfeit of your lives for my sake. Just as I died to set all men free from sin and the devil, many of you will die to water and nourish this new way of life, this new faith with your own blood. But do not be

151

afraid for I will be with you always through my Father's spirit and in here." He touched his heart.

"My love for all of you knows no bounds, and so I will be close to you always, in your hearts as you will be in mine. And some day, when your journey is complete, we will see each other again in my Father's heavenly kingdom, where all the cares of this world will be forgotten, and you will see my Father, and your joy will be both complete and boundless."

Jesus walked toward the table where he had shared two very special meals with his apostles in the last few days. "Come. Sit with me, and let me start to prepare you for your journey. Let me tell you how the Father and I are one and how I will bring you to better know the Father and how you and those who will follow you and their followers for centuries to come will bring my message, my love, to people all around the world."

Lamps were lit as the fourteen men—Jesus, the eleven apostles, Isaac, and Cleopas—took their seats around the table. Outside, darkness was starting to fall over Judea. In this one room, though, the man who would come to be known as the Light of the World started to ignite a new brightness destined to spread and illuminate mankind from this one side street of Jerusalem to the ends of the earth.

The evening of the third day was upon them, but the light inside this room drove away the darkness of the night.

EPILOGUE

It was late afternoon as Joseph of Arimithea slowly paced back and forth in his private study. It had been about ninety days since Jesus had risen from the dead, and much had happened, much of it in front of Joseph's own eyes. Soon after the resurrection, Joseph had left the Sanhedrin and had become a more open follower of Jesus.

He recalled now and treasured the private visit he had with Jesus in which the other man had thanked him for taking care of his mother and for preserving the two artifacts still in his possession—Jesus's crown of thorns and his cup from his last Passover meal with his apostles. Joseph had been amazed Jesus knew of these, particularly the crown of thorns, as he had spoken to no one about them and, in fact, had hidden both of them in his study. But he soon realized there were no secrets when it came to Jesus.

Joseph had also been present when Jesus ascended into heaven, and he was in the room when the gift of which Jesus had spoken, his Father's Spirit, had descended upon all who were in that room. He recalled seeing what looked like tongues of fire come down and touch each of their heads, yet there was no burning other than the one in his own heart and soul as each person was touched by an individual flame. He remembered how the apostles had all begun to speak in a variety of foreign languages and how forceful and bold Peter had been in his subsequent proclamation to the crowd that had gathered outside the building when they heard a noise they all described as a strong wind despite it being a calm day.

Many came to believe in Jesus that day, he thought to himself. *And many more have since then. And I have been privileged—no, that is not the right word. I have been blessed to witness so many of these events.*

He also recalled with some regret how, before Jesus's crucifixion, he had been a disciple in secret because of his position in the Sanhedrin and his fear of his colleagues. He shook his head as he looked back on what now appeared to him to have been cowardice, how he too had abandoned Jesus during his passion and death. And yet the feeling was a fleeting one for it was overpowered by a sense of how he had now made the right choice and how he had been already rewarded for that choice.

He paced some more—slowly, methodically, as his mind whirled, taking in all that had happened in these last hundred days or so. *I have seen so much*, he thought. *I have been so blessed. How can I show my appreciation for what Jesus has done for me? How can I help others to share in the joy and wonder of what I have experienced?* He suddenly stopped pacing, looked over at the desk in the room, and walked toward it. He sat down, reached over, and took a blank parchment scroll from the rack that stood to the right of his desk. He then took a pen, looked up, said a short prayer, and started to write.

"I am a follower of Jesus the Nazorean, who I now know to be the Son of the Living God. I have witnessed many of his acts of kindness and listened to many of his talks to large groups as well as small ones. I was a witness to his torture and death as well as to his rising from the dead and his return to his Father in heaven. I now wish to put down in writing my recollection of these and many other events which I witnessed or heard about from those who were also his followers and witnessed many other events unseen by me. I know them to be true, and I know my own recollections to be true as well, and I wish to share them with those who will follow after us in following him."

He dipped his pen in the ink and continued to write. He wrote long after the sun had set as the light in his room and the one in his heart and mind all continued to burn brightly.

NOTES

1. Standard King James Version Bible. Luke 23: 34
2. Ibid. John 8: 7
3. Ibid. Matthew 6: 34
4. Ibid. John 2: 3
5. Ibid. John 2: 4
6. Ibid. Matthew 16:18
7. Ibid. John 1: 36
8. Ibid. John 1: 38
9. Ibid. John 1: 39
10. Ibid. John 1: 46
11. Ibid. Luke 1: 38
12. Ibid. Luke 1: 48–49
13. Ibid. Isaiah 53: 5–10